"Hilarious and fast-paced, *Mr. Malcolm's List* is a bright and refreshing Regency romp."

—Shelf Awareness

"This is an insightful novel of manners . . . Jane Austen's influence is readily apparent in language usage, character conduct, and, most importantly, the subtle wit and irony that provide so much entertainment."

—Historical Novel Society

"A cheeky look at the different expectations placed on men versus women during the Regency era, revealing the limitations society accords individuals in terms of their family connections and personal wealth and education. Both general fiction readers and romance fans looking for a story that will transport them to another time and place, seeking new fictional friends, or hoping to watch characters grow more self-aware and compassionate will revel in this smart love story."

—*Booklist* (starred review)

"*Miss Lattimore's Letter* is an entertaining romp through historical London, with plenty of romance, humor, and banter that make this a worthwhile read."

—Romance Junkies

"This book is sheer perfection. An adorable, hysterical comedy of manners."

—The Romance Dish

"It was witty and hilarious, and contained a cast of upbeat, brooding, and feisty characters that all graced the page with subtle [*Pride and Prejudice*] undertones. I loved it!"

—The Nerd Daily

The Ladies Rewrite the Rules

SUZANNE ALLAIN

BERKLEY ROMANCE

New York

BERKLEY ROMANCE
Published by Berkley
An imprint of Penguin Random House LLC
penguinrandomhouse.com

Copyright © 2024 by Suzanne Allain
Penguin Random House supports copyright. Copyright fuels creativity,
encourages diverse voices, promotes free speech, and creates a vibrant culture.
Thank you for buying an authorized edition of this book and for complying with
copyright laws by not reproducing, scanning, or distributing any part of it in any
form without permission. You are supporting writers and allowing Penguin
Random House to continue to publish books for every reader.

BERKLEY and the BERKLEY and B colophon are registered
trademarks of Penguin Random House LLC.

Library of Congress Cataloging-in-Publication Data

Names: Allain, Suzanne, author.
Title: The ladies rewrite the rules / Suzanne Allain.
Description: First edition. | New York: Berkley Romance, 2024.
Identifiers: LCCN 2023019650 (print) | LCCN 2023019651 (ebook) |
ISBN 9780593549643 (trade paperback) | ISBN 9780593549650 (ebook)
Subjects: LCGFT: Romance fiction. | Historical fiction. |
Humorous fiction. | Novels.
Classification: LCC PS3601.L398 L34 2024 (print) |
LCC PS3601.L398 (ebook) | DDC 813/.6—dc23/eng/20230428
LC record available at https://lccn.loc.gov/2023019650
LC ebook record available at https://lccn.loc.gov/2023019651

First Edition: January 2024

Printed in the United States of America
1st Printing

In memory of my mother, a true lady,

and in gratitude to my father,

the gentleman who loved her.

1

"YOU HAVE A caller, madam," Godfrey said, in a tone of voice that implied Diana was at fault for this circumstance.

Diana looked up from her needlework in surprise, as it was past visiting hours and so close to dinner that it could only be assumed whoever was calling was angling for an invitation. She turned to look at her companion in confusion and inquiry, but "companion" was an exaggerated description of Mildred, her late husband's sister, who was asleep on the sofa. Mildred was the one thing Diana's wealthy husband had left to her upon his death that she could have happily done without.

"Mildred!" Diana said loudly.

Mildred's head snapped up. "I beg your pardon, but I slept poorly last night. The moon was waxing. Or waning. I always get the terms confused." She blinked a few times, before shaking her head. "Whichever it was, it had quite an effect on the river, and it was roaring ferociously. But I'm sure you heard it yourself . . ."

"I enjoy the sound of the river," Diana said.

"Yes, I know," Mildred said. "Your constitution is unnaturally robust for a widow." She looked reproachfully at Diana, as she often did, as if she knew Diana didn't mourn Mr. Boyle's death sufficiently. Diana found herself almost pleased at the news of an intrusion that she'd previously found annoying, as it gave her an excuse to change the subject.

"We have a caller, Mildred."

"A caller? At this late hour?" Mildred turned to Godfrey, who had stood watching this byplay and was now directing his disgruntled look at her. "Who is it, Godfrey?"

Ignoring Mildred, Godfrey walked over to his mistress, presenting her with the card he held. "Mr. Raymond Pryce," Diana read aloud.

"Never heard of him. Send him away," Mildred said.

Diana had considered doing exactly that, as she had grown so unused to going about in society since her husband's death (not that she had been what one would call gregarious before that), and she was anxious at the thought of entertaining a perfect stranger. Still, she was the mistress of Whitley House, little though Mildred might like it, and she had very few opportunities to exert her authority. So she nervously patted her hair and her dress, took a deep breath, and told Godfrey, "I am at home."

Mildred looked at her as if she had gone mad but said nothing in reply, though she made a clicking sound that signified her disapproval and caused Diana to feel even more pleased with her small act of rebellion.

Godfrey sighed, as if wondering how he'd sunk to serving such a troublesome pair of females, but left to do Diana's bidding. She spent the time while he was gone considering whether it was worth her while to look for a new butler, or if she should continue to employ her late husband's choice. It seemed cruel to reward Godfrey for his many years of service by giving him the sack, but neither did she think that the lady of the house should be intimidated by her own staff, and Diana had always been made to feel as if Godfrey were doing her a favor when he performed even the simplest of his duties.

Her musings were cut short by the entrance into the drawing room of their mysterious caller.

Even though Diana had been married for five very long years and widowed for more than one, she had just recently turned five-and-twenty. However, Mr. Pryce looked even younger than she was, though Diana might have been misled by the fact that his ears were slightly oversized and gave him the appearance of a child who had not yet grown into them. Or it could have been that she had grown so accustomed to Mr. Boyle, who had been fifty-eight years old when he died, that a man of her own age appeared infantile in comparison. But it was not only Mr. Pryce's appearance but also his demeanor that gave the impression of a shy young boy, as he entered the room as if he was afraid of them, darting a quick nervous glance at Mildred before performing a jerky bow.

Diana and Mildred rose at his entrance and bobbed their heads in response to his bow, before Diana gave him permission to sit. His reaction to her command was also very bizarre, as he looked at Diana in surprise, which quickly transformed into delight.

"*You* are Mrs. Boyle?" he asked, smiling tentatively at Diana and looking her up and down—a little too obviously, Diana felt. Mildred must have shared Diana's opinion, as she cleared her throat angrily.

"I am," Diana replied. "Allow me to present you to my sister-in-law, Miss Boyle."

Mr. Pryce looked as if he'd just been informed he'd won a lottery. "Miss Boyle, a pleasure," he said, and he smiled so happily at her that Mildred's own expression lightened reflexively.

They all sat in silence while Mr. Pryce stared at Diana, a grin on his face, and Diana wondered if she was not as socially inept as she had heretofore thought herself because she could never imagine behaving as awkwardly as he was. And while she believed she presented a neat and pleasant appearance, she did not think her charms so great as to cause him to be stricken mute at the sight of her. Diana knew he was most likely comparing her to her older, formidably plain sister-in-law, and so the comparison would inevitably be in her favor.

However, Diana was doing herself an injustice. Having been married at eighteen to a man thirty-five years her senior, she had never had a suitor and so did not realize how attractive she was. Her silky black hair had fallen out of its confines and was in wisps around her face, framing a countenance that was sweet rather than striking. Shy by nature, she frequently cast her eyes downward, so that when she did meet a person's gaze one was struck by the beauty of her large amber-colored eyes with their long dark eyelashes. Certainly, Mr. Pryce had noticed that his hostess was a very lovely young woman.

The silence was growing more and more awkward, their guest apparently having forgotten that he should offer a reason for his call, and so Mildred finally prodded him to do so. "I do not believe we've previously made your acquaintance," she said, her expression having hardened again into its usual rigid lines.

"No, not exactly," Mr. Pryce said. As Diana and Mildred continued staring at him in silent inquiry, he must have finally become conscious of the strained atmosphere, because he stopped grinning and said to Diana: "That is, I am acquainted with a distant relation of your late husband's, and since I was in the vicinity—"

"A relation of mine? Who, pray tell?" Mildred interrupted him to ask.

Mr. Pryce turned to her, a disconcerted expression on his face, as if it had just occurred to him that a relation of Mr. Boyle's would also be related to Mr. Boyle's sister.

"Mr. Cartwright," he finally said, before correcting himself. "That is, Mr. Carter. Or perhaps it was Carnes? Started with a 'Cah' sound, at any rate. It was a brief acquaintance," he mumbled sheepishly, before looking again at Diana, fear writ large in his brown eyes.

Mildred took a deep breath, her bosom expanding impressively, and Diana closed her eyes, as she had begun to pity poor Mr. Pryce, perhaps because of his youthful appearance and his obvious inability to lie. Before the volcano could erupt, however, they were again interrupted by Godfrey.

"Lord Jerome Vincent," he announced, and Mr. Pryce, who had at first seemed to view the butler's appearance in the nature of a deus ex machina, saw who was with him and frowned.

"Good afternoon, Mrs. Boyle," Lord Jerome said, approaching Mildred with a charming smile, though it faltered just a bit when he saw her.

"I am Mrs. Boyle," Diana said, wondering what in the world was happening.

Lord Jerome turned to Diana, and though his countenance gave little away, Diana thought she detected a hint of relief in his sardonic gaze. "I see," he said, and somehow the way he drew out those two words, along with the look that accompanied them, made them seem very suggestive, indeed.

Mr. Pryce pokered up even more at this interchange and said to Lord Jerome, "I might have expected to find you here."

"And why was that?" Lord Jerome asked. Diana and Mildred looked at Mr. Pryce inquiringly as well.

Mr. Pryce flushed a dark red. "No reason," he finally said, and Mildred rolled her eyes and said something under her breath, though the words "half-wit" could be faintly heard.

SOMEHOW THE TWO gentlemen ended up staying for dinner, though Diana wasn't sure how they accomplished it. She felt that she could have overcome Mr. Pryce's feeble attempts to wrangle an invitation, but even Mildred had proved no match for Lord Jerome. He looked to be in his thirties and was neither handsome nor ugly, but had such an air of sophistication that he gave the impression of being much better looking than he actually was.

He was also a very different species of gentleman than Diana had ever before met. Her husband had not been a fixture of London society and had ignored it as determinedly as it ignored him. Even though Whitley House was on the outskirts of town and only a short drive from its myriad entertainments, Diana could count on one hand the number of times she'd been there. Her husband was a quiet, serious, unsociable man, and thus Diana had been forced to live that way as well.

Mr. Boyle had certainly never flirted with her, as Lord Jerome was attempting to do, though Diana responded to many of Lord Jerome's overtures with blank stares and silence. It didn't help that his most outrageous compliments were punctuated by snorts of derision from Mr. Pryce, who spent much of the meal shooting murderous glances at Lord Jerome, interspersed with admiring ones directed at both Diana and her home.

Diana was totally at a loss as to how she'd come to the notice of two of London society's fashionable fribbles. For even though Mr. Pryce was far less sophisticated than Lord Jerome, it was obvious by their familiarity with each other and from Mr. Pryce's clothing, as rumpled as it was, that he was also an inhabitant of that elite sphere.

However, she was not so ignorant as to *why* they were there. While Lord Jerome was much more subtle and did not glance around the room with covetous eyes, instead saving such looks entirely for her person, he had betrayed himself when he had first arrived and directed an appraising look at Mildred, before realizing his mistake.

Both gentlemen were obviously fortune hunters, there on purpose to court a wealthy widow. But how had they even learned of her existence?

Lord Jerome had also claimed, as Mr. Pryce did, to be acquainted with a relative of Mr. Boyle's, but he had had the good sense to say this person's surname was Boyle as well. There were many branches of the Boyle family, as Diana had good reason to know, as she also had been a Boyle before her marriage to her distant cousin. It could even be that Lord Jerome *was* acquainted with a relation of theirs, but Diana found it entirely too coincidental that a chance meeting with a distant relative would spark within both Mr. Pryce and Lord Jerome a desire to call upon her, and on the very same day.

She noticed that Godfrey also appeared perplexed and was watching both men with a furrowed brow, although he directed the serving of dinner in his usual manner, as if it were a chore that was beneath him. Toward the end of the meal, however, while he was removing Diana's plate, he said in a lowered tone, "I have taken the liberty of bringing a bottle of port up from the cellar, ma'am, in anticipation of your wishes."

Diana could only conclude from this statement that he intended to serve after-dinner drinks to her unwelcome guests and wondered why he wished to prolong their visit. But since she knew her butler to be far more au courant than she was, she was not in the least affronted that he'd dropped a hint as to what behavior was expected of her. After all the plates had been removed, she stood up from the table and said: "Miss Boyle and I will retire to the drawing room, but Mr. Pryce and Lord Jerome, do not feel you must join us immediately. We will leave you gentlemen to your port."

Before the men could think of protesting, though it was unlikely that they would have, Godfrey was serving them their drinks and the ladies had left the room.

꧁꧂

"YOU DASTARD!" MR. Pryce said indignantly to Lord Jerome as soon as the door had shut behind Diana.

"Exactly what dastardly behavior on my part are you complaining of?" Lord Jerome asked, though he seemed more interested in watching his port as he swirled it around in his glass than in anything his companion had to say.

"You know perfectly well! You've come to court Mrs. Boyle merely because she's a rich widow."

"Mister Pot, meet Lord Kettle," Lord Jerome said, nodding his head at Mr. Pryce in a mock bow.

Mr. Pryce looked flummoxed for a moment, and then his brow cleared in comprehension. "It's just—I thought everyone else would begin with the *A*'s, and if I skipped to the *B*'s that I'd have the field all to myself. And she's in Twickenham, not in London proper. Didn't expect anyone would want to come all this way."

"Twickenham isn't exactly Timbuktu. That was actually a point in her favor, in my opinion; she has a country house that isn't actually in the country."

"A rather nice house, too," Mr. Pryce said, looking around the dining room appreciatively. But then he seemed to realize he shouldn't be making Mrs. Boyle look even more desirable a prize and hurried to add: "Still, she didn't seem to take to you, so you'd be better off casting your line where the fish are biting."

"Are you likening the beauteous Mrs. Boyle to a fish? Not a very romantic simile, dear chap. Especially when you're a bit of a gudgeon yourself. She wasn't exactly bowled over by your charms," Lord Jerome said, placing an ironic emphasis on the word "charms" as he looked over Pryce in a way that drew attention to all of his sartorial and anatomical deficiencies, and which would have caused a more sensitive man to retire from polite society for a week at least.

Mr. Pryce, however, was unfazed by his dinner companion's supercilious behavior, though it did cause him to notice he'd somehow spilled a bit of gravy on his waistcoat. He rubbed ineffectually at it as he considered why his courting had proven unsuccessful thus far. "Tell you what; I think she's whiddled our scrap."

Lord Jerome wrinkled his nose in distaste. "Must you speak as if you're a denizen of a London rookery? But I concede your point. We may have inadvertently shown our hand."

"'Xactly! Maybe you should cast your peepers over some of the *C*'s."

Godfrey, who was hanging on their every word as surreptitiously as possible and had found this repeated mention of the alphabet very confusing indeed, noticed at this point that Mr. Pryce had pulled a slim booklet out of his waistcoat pocket and was perusing it, before waving it triumphantly in front of Lord Jerome's face. "Here you are: There's a Miss Cavendish with thirty thousand and she lives more convenient to town. Never been married, either, unlike *this* ace of spades," Pryce said, ignoring Lord Jerome's earlier complaint and using a slang term for a widow.

"But I've rather taken a fancy to Mrs. Boyle. Especially now that I've seen her in the, ahem, flesh, so to speak. Why don't *you* make a call on Miss Cavendish?"

The two men proceeded to argue for some time over who should relinquish the field, and Godfrey very generously refilled their glasses as they did so. Much later, he informed the inebriated gentlemen that their hostess had retired for the evening and was sorry she hadn't been able to bid them a good night. Godfrey then saw them both out, putting a helpful arm around Mr. Pryce to steer him toward the door and pocketing the booklet as he did so.

A few minutes later, he handed it to Diana, who had completely changed her mind about terminating her butler's employment and was now considering increasing his salary. She had gone upstairs with Mildred earlier but had returned belowstairs once the men left as she assumed Godfrey would have some information for her. However, she had never expected *this*.

Diana took the booklet from him, reading aloud as she did so: "'*The Rich Ladies Registry or the Batchelor's Directory.*'" She paused for a moment, looking up at Godfrey in shock and dismay, before continuing to read: "'Containing an alphabetical list of the Widows and Spinsters of

Great Britain with an account of their places of abode and reputed fortunes.'"

"You might want to turn over to the 'Widows' section, under the letter *B*, ma'am," Godfrey suggested, and Diana obediently flipped a few pages forward, only to see her name and direction very clearly printed in black and white. A Madam Bechford of Bond Street was listed ahead of Diana, but she had a measly twenty thousand, whereas Madam Boyle of Twickenham was reputed to have a fortune of at least thirty thousand pounds with a few thousand "in the stocks." Diana had no idea if this figure was accurate or not. Her man of affairs had apprised her of her financial standing upon Mr. Boyle's death and she was content to know that her quarterly allowance, which she'd found more than adequate, was to continue, and that if she had need of any more funds, she could apply to him at any time. She had intended to take a more active role in the supervision of the accounts, as she realized ignorance in such matters could lead to disaster, but she also knew appearing too interested in her late husband's wealth would provoke spiteful comments from her sister-in-law, and so she'd resolved to wait a little longer before requesting to examine the situation for herself.

However, it looked as if whoever compiled this directory had done extensive research, so the amount was most likely correct. There were dozens of names, addresses, and figures; the listings for noble widows even stating what their rank and title was, and Diana was dumb-founded at the time and labor the author must have put into compiling such a list. Although it did not appear that alphabetizing was his forte. "He's listed a Madam Baker after me. She should come before," Diana complained, be-fore realizing this was the least of her concerns. "I cannot believe someone would be so encroaching, so intrusive, so . . . despicable! Exposing all the private details of these ladies, without so much as a by-your-leave! Why, it should be against the law to do such a thing! Who is responsible for this?"

That question Godfrey could not answer, so turning back to the title page she read aloud: "'By a Younger Son.' That certainly is specific," she told Godfrey sarcastically. She stared at the front of the booklet in frustration, before flipping another page and realizing there was a dedication addressed "To all Widowers and Batchelors." She resolved to read the dedication carefully when she was alone, but for the moment she merely skipped to the end, and found that the author had signed it: "Your Most Obedient Un-known, M. D—n."

Diana couldn't remember the last time she'd been so angry. Perhaps she never had; she couldn't recall ever hav-ing this much provocation. "So, he has no problem pub-lishing all the ladies' names but he's too shy to publish his own. A little hypocritical of our mysterious Mr. D, wouldn't you say, Godfrey?"

"Indeed. Quite the cad, if I might be permitted to offer an opinion."

"You may, as it corresponds with mine perfectly," Diana said, smiling slightly at Godfrey, who inclined his head in response. He didn't smile back, but she hadn't expected him to. She was beginning to understand him better and now realized that much of her discomfort in his presence was due to the fact that she had been a shy and awkward teen when she'd first met him, not at all the sort of mistress who would inspire respect in a proper butler of three score years. He had also been an eyewitness to her sorry history with Mr. Boyle, something that she was cognizant of whenever she interacted with him. But she was now a mature widow, and it was up to her to set the terms of their relationship. Besides, Godfrey had demonstrated this evening that he could be of assistance to her, and she had need of him.

Because she was going to discover exactly who this dastardly Mr. D was and expose him as publicly as he'd exposed her.

2

Maxwell Dean had seen too many of his friends fall in love with the wrong women.

It wasn't that the ladies were unprincipled or ill-tempered or possessed some other negative character trait that made them unsuitable. No, the obstacle to these matches was one that the women could not be blamed for, but that indisputably made them the wrong choice: they were poor. And while that might not be an impediment for *some* gentlemen, Maxwell and many of his friends were younger sons with no fortune of their own, and thus a poor wife was a luxury that they, quite literally, could not afford.

Max was not in such dire financial straits himself, as he had received his mother's modest dowry as an inheritance; but his income just covered his own expenses. Of course, he was not accustomed to practicing strict economies, and lived the life of a society bachelor with all that it entailed, but children almost inevitably followed marriage, and while he could afford to take care of a wife (though perhaps not in the degree of luxury she might desire), his income could not stretch to include any progeny that might come along. Poets and romantics might rail against a marriage undertaken for anything but love alone, but Max had a more practical view of the matter. He believed that it was just as possible to love a woman of fortune as it was to love a penniless woman; a woman who should be looking elsewhere for a match, as well.

He himself was in no great hurry to wed, though he'd recently begun to think it was time he started looking for a bride. His brother had been married for five years already by the time *he* was eight-and-twenty, Max's current age, and now had four children under the age of six. (Max took a moment to pity his sister-in-law and wonder that since his brother now had an heir, a spare, and two extra for good measure, he didn't leave off breeding for a while.) Maxwell had met his sister-in-law before she'd married his brother, and she'd been the one woman who had inspired Max to consider matrimony. But when she had used her acquaintance with him to pursue his brother instead, Maxwell had learned a valuable lesson about his own eligibility, or lack thereof. He had quickly recovered from any infatuation he had felt for his sister-in-law, but the caution she'd inspired in him about courtship and marriage had remained these past seven years.

Maxwell's thoughts had recently turned again to marriage, not because a certain young lady had captured his fancy, but because he'd witnessed a friend of his, Jack Winston, another younger son, suffer a similar disappointment in love. He and Max had been guests at the wedding breakfast of one of their more fortunate friends, a rich young earl who had had his pick of women and had married a lady whom Jack was enamored of.

"I wish I'd never met her," Jack had muttered sadly, as he watched the couple accept the congratulations of their friends.

Maxwell wondered why Jack had paid court to someone who could never bestow her hand on a man just as poor as she was. Wouldn't it be better, Max reasoned, for younger brothers, like themselves, to confine their attentions to women who could afford to marry them?

And he had been struck by a brilliant notion: What if there were a directory of all the single wealthy women in and near London that younger brothers, such as himself, could peruse before beginning a courtship? It would save any number of young men—and women—the heartache of a doomed love affair.

He had never considered that a lady would not *want* her name in such a directory, supposing that she would be pleased to find herself the object of his friends' attentions, all of them very good chaps. And, he reasoned, the information was accessible to anyone who made an effort to discover it, so it wasn't as if he was revealing anything of a confidential nature.

Perhaps he'd felt some qualms, even if he was not conscious of it, as he had been reluctant to sign his name to the document, limiting himself merely to his initials. But his primary reason for doing so was because he had been rather proud of his work and did not want to be accused of blowing his own trumpet. He never imagined his altruistic action would—instead of accolades—reap scorn, animosity, and blame.

Max was living in rooms in the Albany and could count on one hand the number of times he had received visitors there. He was rarely at home; preferring to spend the day at his club or at his older brother's townhome in Grosvenor Square, where he made frequent use of the library. So he was quite surprised when the porter knocked at his door as he was preparing to leave and informed him he had a caller. The boy handed Max a card, turned down at the corner.

Max read it, but the name meant absolutely nothing to him.

"Should I tell her you're at home, Mister, or would you rather give her the slip?" the porter, Jim, asked in a loud whisper. He apparently assumed Max was involved in a clandestine affair, and though he had never done anything more than bob his head at Max in passing, he was now looking at Max conspiratorially and with newfound respect. As it was usually considered socially unacceptable for a lady to call upon a gentleman, Max wondered if this woman, Mrs. Boyle, was from a lower class of society. She did possess a card, however, which indicated that she was from the middle classes, at least. Mysteries like these didn't present themselves on his doorstep every day, and Max's curiosity was roused.

"I will receive the lady," Max said, as grandly as he could, in an attempt to deflate Jim's impertinence. It was a wasted effort, however, because the boy merely nodded and winked, as if he had now been made an equal partner in whatever intrigue was taking place.

Max looked around his sitting room, picking up a discarded cravat from the night before and hurling it through the open door into his bedroom. He closed the bedroom door just as the porter returned.

"Madam and her maid to see you," Jim announced in a carrying tone of voice. He apparently had ambitions of becoming a butler. Max just hoped his neighbors were not at home to overhear this pronouncement and discover he was entertaining a woman in his rooms.

The two women entered, and Max nodded his head at Jim in dismissal, as he seemed disposed to linger. The boy finally left, casting curious and admiring glances at Mrs. Boyle as he did so. Now that Max had seen her for himself, he could understand why Jim had assumed there to be some mystery involved with their meeting. She was dressed from head to toe in unrelieved black and had a lace veil draped over her bonnet. However, even though her face was somewhat obscured, it was obvious from what could be seen of it and of her figure that she was a young woman, not an elderly crone, despite her choice of attire.

That she was a lady Maxwell no longer doubted; the very fact that she'd veiled herself and was accompanied by a maid showed that she understood she was breaking a social taboo and did not want to be recognized while doing so. But if she was also attempting to conceal her attractions, she had failed; the glimpses Max caught of her features through the lace caused him to suddenly wish that the porter's suppositions were correct and that he did have a romantic relationship with the lady. Provided she was a widow, of course.

Max's captivation was complete when she lifted her veil, exposing the loveliest countenance he'd ever seen. Or at least it seemed that way to him, though her full lips were compressed tightly, and her golden-brown eyes seemed to spark with an angry light.

"Mr. Dean? Mr. Maxwell Dean?" she asked, and though she spoke in a firm tone, it struck a discordant note when uttered in her soft voice.

"At your service," Maxwell replied, with a bow and a wide smile. Mrs. Boyle seemed surprised at his cordial response and paused, so Max took the opportunity to invite her to take a seat. She looked further confused—apparently she hadn't planned on making a long visit—but finally sat gingerly on the edge of a chair. It was obvious she did not want to make herself *too* comfortable.

Max sat on the sofa across from her, after directing her maid to a seat in the corner.

"Mr. Dean," the lady said, fumbling in the reticule she carried and pulling out a sheaf of papers. "I believe you're the author of this *document*, are you not?" She pronounced "document" with a distinct curl of her pretty lips, as if it were an obscene word.

Max was astounded to see she was holding his directory, and it never even occurred to him to try to deny authorship. "Why, however did you discover that?"

"It's true, then? You admit you are its author?" Mrs. Boyle asked.

Her attitude was beginning to affect Max, and his welcoming smile faded in the face of such obvious hostility. "It is not a crime, Mrs. Boyle, and neither is this a court of law. I have no hesitation in admitting I prepared that document, though I am at a loss as to why you are in my rooms demanding that I do so."

"Well, Mr. Dean, I would never want to discompose *you* in any way, so allow me to make it completely clear why I had the audacity to violate *your privacy* by appearing, without warning *or permission*, in your rooms," Mrs. Boyle said, her tone fairly dripping with sarcasm. She then flipped a few pages forward in the directory and stood up to walk over to where he sat on the sofa.

Max jumped to his feet immediately (as a gentleman he couldn't remain seated while she was not), but he had finally understood the source of her displeasure during her accusatory speech, even though he hadn't initially recognized her name. There were dozens of ladies listed in his directory, so he couldn't be expected to remember every one.

And at the moment he could barely remember his *own* name, so close was she standing to him. Apparently she wanted there to be no possibility of his missing what had so enraged her, and was therefore holding the directory right in front of his face. Her proximity was causing him to feel short of breath, and he looked unseeingly at the page for a long moment as she waited, her finger pointing to the relevant entry. Her skirts were brushing his leg and a faint scent of lavender wafted up to him from her person, and he had great difficulty marshaling his thoughts. He was not sure how long they stood there in silence—it might have been seconds or minutes, it felt like time was both rushing by and standing still—until the maid sneezed and broke the spell that had held them in thrall. Mrs. Boyle finally stepped away, and after she'd resumed her seat, Max dropped back down onto the sofa.

"Well? Have you nothing to say?" Diana asked indignantly, though she'd had to stoke her anger by reminding herself how despicable Mr. Dean was and what a terrible thing he'd done. She hadn't thought much about what her archenemy would look like, except to suppose that his outward appearance would be in keeping with his fiendish character. However, this was one of the most attractive men it had ever been her misfortune to meet. His hair was neither light nor dark but had shades of both and fell in disordered waves above gray-blue eyes. Nor was he an oily, uncouth oaf; his manners were pleasing, and his smile had caused an unfamiliar tingling sensation in her stomach. His rooms, while simply and sparsely decorated, were clean, as was his person, and when they'd been standing so close to each other, she'd been amazed at the feeling that seemed to have sparked between them, an exhilarating tension she'd never before experienced.

But she reminded herself that the devil himself could transform into an angel of light, and that she had absolutely no interest in men, even handsome ones. *Especially* handsome ones.

"I gather you're not happy about your inclusion in this document," Mr. Dean said mildly, as if it were a trifling matter. Diana was pleased by this response, because of how greatly it *displeased* her. She no longer had to pretend she was angry; her anger had returned in full measure.

"Not happy? *Not happy?* That might be the most egregious understatement I've ever heard in my life! Would you be happy to find perfect strangers on your doorstep, angling for a dinner invitation, in pursuit of a wealthy bride?"

"Did that happen to you?" Maxwell asked, surprised.

"What did you expect to happen when you published my bank balance, marital status, and direction for the world to see?" Diana said, congratulating herself on having finally brought the man to a realization of his shameless behavior.

"I sincerely beg your pardon for the inconvenience, Mrs. Boyle, but couldn't you simply have told them you were not at home?"

Since this was an unanswerable question, Diana didn't attempt to reply, but returned to the main point of the discussion: "Why would you do such a thing, Mr. Dean, without first asking permission?"

"It just never occurred to me . . . I mean, I thought I was performing a service . . ." His sentence trailed off, and he ran his hand nervously through the wavy hair that fell on his forehead, before beginning again. "Impoverished young ladies come out in society every year with the obvious intention of finding a rich man to marry, and I thought, 'What's sauce for the goose—'"

"Please tell me you aren't using a nursery rhyme to justify your behavior!" Diana interrupted him.

"It's a respected proverb," Mr. Dean said defensively.

"That a man wrote!" Diana replied.

There was a chuckle, quickly suppressed, from the corner, and Mr. Dean and Diana looked over at the maid, surprised to be reminded yet again that they were not alone.

"Beg pardon, ma'am," the girl said, and gave a fake cough. "Had a tickle in my throat." Diana thought it was a good thing Sally had no ambition to take up a career on the stage, because she was a terrible actress.

But the interruption had given Mr. Dean an opportunity to gather his defenses. "Mrs. Boyle, haven't you ever known someone who was the victim of an ill-fated love affair? Who gave their heart to someone to whom they could not offer their hand? It would spare so much heartache if one could know before embarking on a courtship if it had any hope of succeeding."

"I do not feel a marriage based on how much money a person has in the bank has much hope of succeeding in any case," Diana said, grateful she was able to form a coherent response. She felt it very unfair that she had to argue with a man who spoke so passionately and eloquently about love, and who was so annoyingly attractive while doing so.

"Is that so? Can you tell me then, with no pang of conscience, that you married your husband purely for the sake of sentiment, with absolutely no consideration of his financial situation? If you can, then I will cease publication of my directory immediately, and even try to retrieve as many copies as I can of those that have already been purchased."

Diana looked down, seemingly unable to meet Mr. Dean's challenging gaze, before rising from her seat and gesturing to Sally. The girl got up and crossed to stand behind her mistress. Mr. Dean rose from his seat as well, and Diana, who had regained her composure, looked him straight in the eye.

"I have no need to tell you anything, Mr. Dean," she said, holding out her hand to him.

He was surprised, but reached out to grasp her hand, thinking she had offered it to him to shake. However, when his hand touched hers, she jumped back as if she'd been scalded.

"I merely desired you to return my property," she said, a little breathlessly, and he realized he still held the directory.

"Oh, of course," he said, and was too gentlemanly to taunt her for asking for the despised document or inquire as to why she wanted it. He gave it to her and she turned to leave, her maid trailing at her heels.

"Wait!" Max called suddenly, and she paused in the doorway and looked back at him, raising her eyebrows in inquiry. "I *am* sorry, Mrs. Boyle, for offending you. I had no desire to cause anyone . . ." He paused for a moment, searching for the correct word. ". . . *distress* when publishing that directory. Quite the opposite, in fact."

She nodded regally, as if she wished to acknowledge his apology without signifying her acceptance of it. "Unfortunately, I am not the only person to whom you owe an apology, Mr. Dean," she said, and quickly left the room. Sally, who was not quite as swift as Mrs. Boyle, in more ways than one, stood gaping at Max for a moment before she followed her mistress into the hallway and closed the door behind them.

Max stood there, staring at the closed door, conscious that Mrs. Boyle had left a faint hint of her perfume behind to torment him with the thought that the amorphous scent was as fleeting and unattainable as she was.

DIANA HAD TAKEN a suite at the Clarendon Hotel, which was a short walk from the Albany, made even shorter by the brisk, angry pace she set when leaving Mr. Dean's rooms. She was eventually forced to slow down, however, as Sally was falling too far behind, and the foot and carriage traffic was increasing considerably.

She waited impatiently for the maid to catch up, and then made a conscious effort to walk more slowly the rest of the way. She had already defied convention once that day by bearding a single gentleman in his rooms; she had no wish to call attention to herself by taking manly strides instead of mincing ladylike steps.

After entering the Clarendon and going to her suite, she changed from her black dress and bonnet into a sprigged muslin, relieved to be out of her widow's garb. Her mourning period had ended only a few months previously and wearing so much black had made her feel like a hypocrite, as she was conscious that she did not grieve for her husband as much as a good wife ought. Indeed, she did not grieve his death at all, try as she did to think well of him.

She would remind herself that, though at times he had been unkind and ill-tempered, he had never actually abused her; in fact, his offer to marry her had removed her and her mother from a desperate situation after the death of Diana's father. Finding themselves penniless and about to be cast out of their lodgings, they had approached Mr. Boyle, whom they had never met but who was a distant cousin of Diana's father, and the only one of his relatives they'd been able to locate. Mr. Boyle had come up with the notion of marrying Diana in order to give her and her mother a home. (Diana never referred to Mr. Boyle by his Christian name, even in her thoughts.) Diana's mother had repeatedly told her how grateful she should be that a man of means wanted to marry her, providing her with wealth and security, something Diana's mother had never had. However, Diana had had the mutinous thought, though unexpressed, that if Mr. Boyle had truly been motivated by charitable feelings, he would have proposed marriage to her mother instead, who was, after all, closer to him in age than Diana, while still twelve years his junior. Or, barring that, Mr. Boyle could have provided them with a home, or assisted them in finding one, without requiring either of his female relatives to marry him.

Instead it was Diana's duty to sacrifice herself on the

marriage altar, and perhaps it had been the better plan, as her mother was dead within a few weeks of the ceremony.

Diana, grief-stricken by her mother's death, found no comfort in the arms of a man born a decade before her father. She also found her new duties as chatelaine of a large estate at the tender age of eighteen a very unwelcome and difficult burden. It would have been challenging even at the best of times, as she had been raised in a modest dwelling in Plymouth, the daughter of an improvident sailor, and had never been trained to manage a grand household. But it was almost too much to bear when she was forced to assume such duties, as well as live as a wife to a man who was a stranger to her, while trying to cope with the tragic loss of her mother, who had been her constant companion and the mainstay of her young life.

As unhappy as those years had been and as much as she'd wished she'd been able to find a different solution, she could no longer regret her marriage, as she had grown very fond of Whitley House (however little she might feel for its master), and with her husband's death had achieved the independence her poor mother, and so many other women, never possessed. Diana no longer needed a *man* to provide her with food, clothing, and shelter; she had all of that and more.

There was absolutely no reason for her to marry again and she had no intention of doing so. Why give up the independence she had endured so much to attain? And why give away ownership of her beloved Whitley House, which she had finally learned to manage very well, to a charming wastrel like her father, or a bad-tempered auto-crat like her late husband?

The visit of Mr. Pryce and Lord Jerome had merely strengthened her determination never to wed again. She saw how they viewed her: as a necessary evil in the way of their possession of her house and fortune. Of course, she realized that they had found her handsome (at least hand-somer than her poor sister-in-law, which was not necessar-ily a compliment). And the very fact that they had looked Mildred over first made their true priorities evident.

Diana had imagined if she told Mr. Dean how he'd wronged her, it would calm her and she could continue with her placid existence at Whitley House, working in the gardens and decorating the rooms and calling on the few friends she'd made since her marriage. But she found herself even more agitated after her brief visit to Mr. Dean.

Godfrey had been able to track down Mr. Dean's iden-tity after visiting the publisher of the directory, whose ad-dress was printed on the title page. Diana, grateful for Godfrey's help, had considered asking him to accompany her when she confronted Mr. Dean, but after further thought decided to take Sally instead. Though Godfrey had proved himself helpful in this affair, Diana was still ill at ease in his presence. He seemed to be too observant, to see too much. She would have felt much more nervous conversing with Mr. Dean had Godfrey been there. Even Sally, with her sneezes and snickers, disturbed her far less than Godfrey did with his silent disdain.

She did wonder, though, what Godfrey would have thought of Mr. Dean had he accompanied her. Diana, though she'd expected to detest the gentleman, found it difficult to do so and was annoyed with herself for letting his good looks affect her opinion of him. Although it was not merely how he looked; he'd had such an appealing way about him as well. Then again, she had made a call on him instead of him upon her. If he had come to Whitley House in a blatant attempt to pursue her as the other two men had, surely she would have recoiled in horror from him as well. However, Mr. Dean had no need to go to Twickenham; there were dozens of women listed in his directory, and he had probably already begun courting a different young lady who lived close by. The thought of Mr. Dean taking some poor young woman totally unaware, flashing that charming smile at her in a devious attempt to separate her from her fortune, riled Diana to anger once again.

She sat down at the escritoire in her suite at the Clarendon and began writing to the ladies in Mr. Dean's directory.

3

DIANA HAD NO intention of staying at the Clarendon for more than a week; it was far too expensive and she had been poor for too many years to enjoy such luxury without keeping a mental ledger of what it was all costing her. But she needed a convenient place to invite the women in the directory to call on her, and many of them lived in the West End.

Of course, Diana could have called upon them all herself, but it would have taken her an inordinate amount of time; several days, if not weeks. No, the logical thing to do was to invite the group to attend her here, where she could inform them all at the same time of the despicable scheme that was afoot.

She had no desire to make any sort of social debut or to insert her unwelcome self into London society. She had no connections in the *haut ton* and no social ambitions.

Since arriving in town, she'd even regretted her choice of hotel, as luxurious as it undoubtedly was, once she'd discovered how many of the nobility were among its patrons. She ate all her meals in her own suite and was made very uncomfortable by the notice she attracted whenever she passed through the public areas.

Diana had not invited Mildred to accompany her as Diana had reasoned that she was a respectable widow, not a young debutante making her come-out, and she did not need a chaperone, whatever Mildred herself might think. But Diana did wonder if she'd have been the object of less curiosity if she'd had an older lady with her. Then again, Mildred's chief joy in life was complaining, and she would have undoubtedly found some way of loudly doing so and attracting notice to them both, so having Mildred with her would have been no guarantee of anonymity.

The proprietor of the Clarendon, a French gentleman by the name of Monsieur Jacquier, had been of great assistance in reserving a private room for Diana to receive the ladies she'd invited to call on her. The meeting was to be held on Friday morning, though she had no idea how many of the twenty she'd invited would accept her invitation. It had been a difficult letter to compose; there were so many to be copied and sent that she had written only a few sentences, while still attempting to convey the importance and delicacy of the matter she wished to discuss. She hoped she'd struck the correct tone, but after the letters were dispatched she realized her words could be misconstrued a dozen different ways, and the recipients might assume her to be anything from a social climber to a blackmailer. However, Diana quickly reassured herself that this was one reason to be glad she was staying at this very proper hotel on Bond Street: the ladies had to be aware that a petty thief could never afford these prices.

Diana was quite nervous at the prospect of meeting even a few ladies she was unacquainted with, never mind the twenty she'd invited, and began to hope, somewhat perversely, that none of them would come.

There were at least fifty women listed in the directory, but Diana had confined the invitations to those living nearest to her hotel, thinking they would be the most likely to accept. She also assumed they would be the most obvious targets of Mr. Dean and his peers, living in the middle of fashionable London as they did. She was somewhat surprised that Mr. Pryce and Lord Jerome had ventured outside of town to meet her, but she imagined she had stood out since she was the only lady listed who lived in Twickenham, and for all Diana knew they had already tried their luck with the ladies in their own circle.

She dressed carefully for the meeting in an attempt to boost her confidence, and Sally, as careless as she might be about many things, was a very good dresser. She and Diana decided together on a white muslin morning dress paired with a spencerette of rose-colored velvet and a lacy cornette ornamented with flowers to wear on her head. Her gloves were lemon-colored, and whenever she peeked down at them, the bright, happy color immediately raised her spirits.

However, Diana's heart sank down to her pale pink slippers when her first guest was introduced, as she'd never seen such a vision of elegance in her life, and felt she must look very provincial, indeed, compared with this rich society lady.

"Mrs. Boyle?" the woman asked, coming to stand in front of Diana and looking at her very haughtily. Diana nodded, thinking the gesture would answer the lady's question while also doubling as a polite greeting. "I am Lady Regina Townsend," the lady said, returning Diana's nod with an infinitesimal inclination of her head.

Lady Regina was the daughter of a marquess, and one of the highest-ranking ladies on the list. When Diana had seen her name, she'd felt Mr. Dean must have been out of his mind to include her; surely Lady Regina would not look twice at a younger son and had no need of suitors.

Though now that Diana had met her, she realized Lady Regina was somewhat old to still be unmarried, which the directory claimed her to be, as her entry was in the "Spinsters" section. She looked to be in her late twenties, had light brown hair and blue eyes, but was not conventionally pretty; her nose was a trifle too wide and her chin somewhat pointed. However, she had such an air about her that Diana felt any observer would immediately classify her as a beauty, whether it was true or not.

Before Diana could do anything other than thank Lady

Regina for coming, another lady had arrived. A few minutes later there were a dozen women in the room, some of whom were already well acquainted. There were exclamations of "You received an invitation as well?" and "But what is it all about? I almost didn't come." Though most appeared to be in their twenties, there was one lady who looked to be in her mid-thirties and another on the shady side of forty.

Diana cleared her throat as loudly as she could and eventually the chatter died out and the ladies turned to look at her. "Thank you for coming," Diana said, willing her voice not to squeak. She hoped that she didn't sound as nervous as she felt. "If you would please take a seat, I will explain why I invited you here."

The ladies obediently sat down, though the door opened just then and another woman entered. However, seeing the program had already begun she took a seat right away, and after a moment Diana began speaking again. "All of you, as well as myself, are listed in a directory of rich young women, printed for the sole purpose of acquainting impoverished gentlemen with our information, so that they can court us and eventually wed us for our money."

There was a shocked gasp, and Diana found that her nervousness was beginning to dissipate. "Were any of you already aware of this?" she asked.

There were cries of "No," "What effrontery!" and "I had no idea!" accompanied by shakes of the head.

"I think it's obvious that none of us had any knowledge

of such a thing; I know I did not," Lady Regina said, having apparently appointed herself the group's spokeswoman. She glanced around the room to confirm her statement and found all the ladies nodding in agreement. "Pray continue," she told Diana. "How did you discover such a document exists?"

"I obtained a copy," Diana said. She took the directory out of the drawer where she had placed it before the meeting began and held it up for them to see. She hadn't hidden it for dramatic effect, but because she had not wanted any of the ladies to see it until she'd had a chance to explain what it was. However, no stage performer could have received a more satisfying reaction from an audience. There were again gasps of shock, and each woman instinctively leaned in closer to Diana, their attention riveted on what she held.

"Two young gentlemen I'd never before met called on me, and my butler was able to procure this from them," Diana explained. "A Lord Jerome Vincent and a Mr. Raymond Pryce. Have any of you begun receiving calls from mysterious gentlemen?"

Lady Regina, whose reaction hadn't been quite as intense as the rest of the women's when she'd learned of the directory, her aristocratic mask still firmly in place, did look startled when she heard the men's names, but Diana had no chance to question her as one of the other women started speaking.

"I met a nice gentleman just last week, at Gunter's. I dropped some of my ice on his boot, and we discovered we had an acquaintance in common. He called on me again this morning, just before I came here. You don't think he somehow *arranged* our meeting . . ." she said, her voice trailing off in dismay at the thought.

"There's no way of knowing," Diana said. "That is why I wanted to make each of you aware of the directory, so you could be on guard."

The room again disrupted into chatter before Lady Regina silenced everyone again. This time, however, she did so with a laugh.

Everyone stopped talking and turned to look at her, wondering at her odd reaction.

"Why, this is wonderful!" she said, smiling brightly and managing to look pretty, rather than coldly elegant, with her features transformed for the first time into a pleasant expression. "Don't you see? It changes everything."

Diana wasn't the only lady confused, and so Lady Regina hopped up from her seat to stand next to Diana. "May I?" she asked Diana politely.

"Please," Diana responded, taking the seat Lady Regina had vacated and relinquishing the floor to her.

"I'm sure this is not the first time some of you have been prey to fortune hunters," Lady Regina said, looking carefully around and locking gazes with many of the ladies, who nodded in reply. "Of course, if you are a rich man's widow, perhaps this *is* a new experience, but if you were raised as I was, an heiress to a large fortune, you have been pursued since you put up your hair, if not earlier.

And even though that was the case, you were still taught *you* had to be agreeable to *them*; dance with them, but not too close; flirt with them, but not too much; smile at them, but not too often. Well, this is our chance to hold a position of power. Let them dance to *our* tune is what I say."

There was one call of "Hear, hear!" but most of the ladies just looked confused.

"Instead of cowering in fear and locking ourselves away from these men, why not embrace our role?" Lady Regina continued. "After all, we now possess the upper hand. Think of all of us at eighteen, rigorously conforming to society's many rules for women, while these *noble* gentlemen could engage in all kinds of nefarious conduct, which didn't even get them barred from Almack's assemblies, as long as they were *punctual*," she said, her voice dripping with scorn.

There was a slight pause, and then the lady in her thirties suddenly spoke. "I just realized who you are. You're Lady Regina Townsend, are you not?"

"I am," Lady Regina replied, staring defiantly back at her. "I recognize you as well, Mrs. Seymour."

A few of the ladies looked as puzzled as Diana at this interchange, but it seemed as though most of them recognized Lady Regina's name and some disapproved of her as strongly as Mrs. Seymour did. This was made obvious when both Mrs. Seymour and another lady got up and walked out of the room.

"Good riddance!" the elegant lady who looked to be in

her forties announced, before smiling kindly at Lady Regina. "They obviously haven't the backbone for your plan. Now please, finish explaining exactly what it is," she encouraged Lady Regina.

Lady Regina looked for a moment as if she couldn't continue, so taken aback was she by the unexpected support of the older woman. But though her eyes welled up with tears at this act of kindness, she blinked them away and took a deep breath before saying, "Thank you, Lady Gordon." Diana remembered seeing Lady Gordon listed as a widow and a baroness.

"So," Lady Regina said briskly, having pulled herself together, "I propose that we make it clear that we are aware of this document, and allow the gentlemen to exert themselves to please us, in a reverse of what generally occurs during the London season, where we are the ones seeking suitable mates. Let *them* meet *our* requirements, for once, and fear being cast out of our society, or of displeasing us in any way."

"But what if we do not wish to marry?" Diana asked, much more loudly and stridently than she'd intended. The women around her all turned to look at her in surprise.

"Why, what other option is there?" one of the younger ladies asked.

Lady Regina was looking at Diana in sympathy. "Then don't. That's the beauty of it: we can choose to trifle with their affections as much as we like, the same way they do with ours. We have the power. They've granted it to us by means of our inclusion on this list. We are . . . 'The Ladies of the Registry,'" she announced, with a triumphant smile, gesturing toward the directory that Diana still held, where the title, *The Rich Ladies Registry or the Batchelor's Directory*, could be seen.

Diana thought about making Mr. Dean dance to *her* tune and felt a tingle of excitement at the prospect.

"And we'll begin by throwing a ball," Lady Regina said.

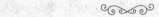

THE ELEVEN WOMEN who remained were introduced to one another, though nine of them were already acquainted, as they traveled in the same exalted circles. It was only Diana and a Miss Jarmyn who were unknown to the rest. Diana passed the directory around the room, and they divided the remainder of the names among themselves, each being assigned to contact two or three others. They excused Diana from having to contact anyone else, however, as she'd already done more than her fair share.

Diana was happy to relinquish control to the much more confident Lady Regina. She was still not sure that she completely grasped or even agreed with her plan; Diana didn't understand how she would be avenging herself on Maxwell Dean by allowing him to woo her.

But that didn't mean she didn't find the prospect exciting, indeed.

4

Diana's mother had educated her at home, at a rickety table in their small, dilapidated cottage, as there was no money to spare for schools or governesses (though she had scraped together enough money when Diana was fourteen to send her to a day school for a few months). French was one of the subjects Susannah Boyle had taught her daughter, even though she had to have known it was inconceivable that Diana would ever have the money for jaunts to Paris, and Susannah's own French was merely passable. Still, she had wanted Diana educated as she had been, in that long ago time when she hadn't had to launder her own clothes, clean her own house, and have bone broth for dinner five nights out of seven. And one possession Susannah had kept from her former life, as it wouldn't have profited her to sell it, was a book of French fairy tales.

It had been a long time since Diana had thought about

those stories her mother had read to her, but her current situation reminded her of one: that of the sleeping beauty in the woods. Diana hadn't been cursed to sleep for a hundred years as the princess had, but she did feel as though the last seven years of her life she'd been merely existing, and that she'd finally been awoken from her metaphorical slumber. It was no longer a matter of merely enduring the long days, weeks, months, and years, but instead she now greeted each new day with excitement and anticipation.

She didn't like to think too much, however, about the fact that if she were the sleeping princess, that meant Mr. Dean was filling the prince's role, and his method of awakening her was far from chivalrous. When she reached that point in her meditations, she would dismiss the entire notion. It was just a fairy tale, after all, and it was ridiculous to try to find parallels in it to her own situation.

Especially since she hadn't even seen Mr. Dean since she'd visited him in his rooms, and it was an entirely different relationship that was enlivening her days. Because, for the first time since her mother's death, she had a sympathetic companion, a true friend. And it was someone she would never have imagined would befriend her: the aristocratic Lady Regina Townsend. Though after a few days Diana had been invited to dispense with her title, and they were now both calling each other by their first names.

Regina had visited Diana again at the Clarendon the day after they'd met, to discuss the arrangements for their ball. That led to a shopping expedition together, and an invitation for Diana to have tea with Regina at her town-home. Over the next week they'd seen each other every day, and Diana was very sorry when the time came for her to say goodbye. She asked Regina to call on her at Whitley House, even inviting her to make an extended stay.

"I would enjoy that, Diana," Regina replied, "but must you really leave town? I know your home is no more than an hour away, but that is so inconvenient when you and I have so much to talk about and plan together. Why don't you stay here, with me? At least until after the ball. Please say that you will! I could show you the London attractions you haven't had time to see, and we could visit the theatre together. You've never been to the theatre, have you?"

"Never," Diana said, touched by Regina's eagerness for her company. Diana had decided to return to Whitley House because she could not justify staying at an expensive hotel indefinitely when her own home was so near, but there was really nothing that made it necessary for her to return home immediately. She certainly didn't miss Mildred's so-called company. She could go to Twicken-ham tomorrow, pack a few more things, and give instructions to the housekeeper before returning to stay with Regina. And staying with a friend was a much more pleasant prospect than staying with a maid at a hotel, even if it was the Clarendon. But just when she was about to accept the invitation, Regina's happy, eager expression faded and she grew serious.

"Before you decide whether or not you'll stay—and I would like nothing better, I assure you—I must first warn you of the consequences."

Diana waited in fraught silence as Regina nervously clasped and unclasped her hands before raising her chin defiantly and saying, "You see, Diana, I am no longer accepted in polite society. They consider me . . . unvirtuous." Regina's haughty tone had faltered by the end of her statement, and she was no longer able to meet Diana's eyes. She continued in a tone of voice that was barely audible, and Diana had to lean in closer to hear her. "I probably should have warned you at the start of our acquaintance, an association with me will most likely prevent your being accepted by the *haut ton*, as well. I suppose I was too excited to have a friend who knew nothing of my past and did not look at me with contempt. I beg your pardon for saying nothing before now."

Diana grasped one of Regina's fluttering hands. "There is nothing to apologize for. While I appreciate the warning, I've never aspired to be part of London society, and I am perfectly content with yours."

Regina squeezed the hand that held hers before releasing it. She seemed more at ease now that she'd confided her secret, and smiled a little mischievously at Diana as she refilled both their teacups. "Perhaps that is why I wasn't as offended by my inclusion on this list as you were. I'm sure I should have reacted as angrily as you did at Mr. Dean's presumption, but frankly, I was just so surprised—

and pleased—that he didn't consider me unworthy of making a respectable marriage, that it was difficult for me to take offense."

"Perhaps I overreacted. I'm sure if my first marriage had been different, I would not have been so affronted."

Regina shook her head. "No, it was certainly wrong of Mr. Dean to do such a thing, and if you hadn't gotten wind of it and warned the rest of us, we could have been deceived by some unscrupulous young men. But 'knowledge itself is power' as the saying goes, and thanks to you, we ladies now have the upper hand."

They were silent for a moment, and Diana wondered if Regina would confide more fully in her. Diana was still unused to exchanging confidences; she had kept her own counsel for so many years, and so had not told Regina about her own unhappy marriage, other than to imply that she'd been less than content. And she didn't require any explanation from her friend; she'd learned enough about Regina to believe she *was* virtuous, in every sense that mattered, and assumed that Regina had been the victim of gossip or even slander. Surely, Diana reasoned, if Regina weren't a trustworthy, *principled* person, she wouldn't have issued any warning at all.

Regina's thoughts must have been following a similar pattern because she abruptly said, "I suppose you'd appreciate an explanation of why I'm a social pariah."

Diana shook her head vigorously. "No, Regina, you need explain nothing to me. Even though we have known each other only a short time, I've learned enough about you to know such rumors must be false, or at least exaggerated."

Regina sighed. "I wish I could claim there was absolutely no truth in the accusation, but I must admit that I was guilty of some misbehavior."

"All of us have said or done things we later regret. That does not mean they should be held against us for the rest of our lives."

Regina nodded in agreement, but to Diana's horror, a tear coursed its way down her cheek. "Now I've upset you! I'm so sorry," Diana said, setting her cup down and awkwardly holding out her hand.

"No, not at all. Quite the opposite," Regina assured her, wiping the tear away. "You said nothing I have not been telling myself for the last eleven years. It happened so long ago, when I was barely more than seventeen, and it does seem unfair that I must continue to pay the price for my youthful folly, especially when a man can do far worse with impunity."

Diana made a gesture of agreement but did not speak, and Regina left her seat to go stand by the window before continuing her story.

"My father had arranged a marriage for me with the son of a family friend when I was fifteen. And while I had no particular complaint about the groom—to be perfectly honest, I was more than a little enamored of him—I did resent the fact that I was to miss out entirely on a courtship. My fiancé treated me as if I were his younger sister, and there was not a hint of *romance* in our relationship. So when another gentleman appeared—though I flatter him by calling him such—and gave me all the compliments my silly, immature heart desired, I was easily persuaded to meet him clandestinely, and eventually to run away with him to Gretna Green."

Regina turned to look directly at Diana, a rueful smile on her face. "As I am still a spinster, you cannot fail to realize that both marriages came to naught."

Though Diana was surprised that Regina had eloped with a man and hadn't married him, she attempted to hide it. "Undoubtedly that was for the best," she responded to her friend's disclosure.

Regina shrugged. "Perhaps. I am not at all sorry I was prevented from marrying my erstwhile suitor, at any rate, as I came to my senses very early in our journey, and was never so relieved in my life as when my father found us at the inn we'd stopped at that first night. But it was too late. Oh, nothing untoward happened," Regina assured Diana, as Diana could not completely hide her fearful expression at the thought of what her friend might have suffered. "He was not quite unscrupulous enough to force himself upon me, and was probably not at all eager to, in any event, as I doubt he was as stricken with my charms as he had implied," Regina said, with a self-deprecating smile. "However, I was still ruined, in rumor if not in fact, as it was the middle of the night by the time my father arrived, and we'd been alone together since the previous day. Plenty of time for something to *have* happened, and there was no doubt in anyone's mind that something did. And we were so unfortunate as to stay at an inn that was also housing a voracious gossip who had seen me there, unchaperoned, so there was no hope of hushing the thing up. Indeed, at that point my father tried to convince me *to* marry the man, but I staunchly refused and begged to be returned home. Father did pay him off in an attempt to keep the affair quiet, but I doubt whether it would have mattered if he had done so or not, as there was no amount of money he could offer that would silence the others who had witnessed my disgrace."

"But what about the man to whom you'd been affianced? Surely he wasn't such a cad as to jilt you after you'd explained your innocence?" Diana asked.

"I don't know whether he would have stood by me or not, as I had already sent him a letter breaking the engagement the day before my elopement. How could I then tell him that I had mistaken my feelings, and now that I was considered 'damaged goods' and a social outcast that I would be pleased to marry him, after all?" Regina shook her head. "Perhaps there was a way we could have been reconciled, but I was too humiliated to even attempt it, and knew not how to do so. And my father and brother were so enraged by my actions that they refused to intervene on my behalf. I only saw my former fiancé again almost a year later, after I'd come to London, and it was clear he did not intend to acknowledge our relationship.

And even if I had not jilted him, when I saw how I was treated when I attempted to enter society, I would not have expected him to approach me. Only the most flagrant of fortune hunters and rakes did so, and I could have happily done without their attentions. I only stayed a few weeks before calling it quits and returning to the country."

"Oh, Regina, I'm so sorry."

"So am I. When I think of how one stupid decision altered the entire course of my life . . ." Her voice trailed off, but then she seemed to make an effort to lighten the mood, straightening her shoulders and walking back to sit near Diana with her head held high. "But then, there's no point in regrets," she said, smiling determinedly.

"No point at all," Diana agreed.

RATHER THAN PUTTING a damper on the two women's growing friendship as she had apparently feared it might, Regina's confession only served to strengthen it. Though she and Diana were considered "rich" and were the possessors of sizable fortunes, they had felt themselves anything *but* fortunate, as empty and lonely as their lives had been. But they both couldn't help feeling they were on the brink of a new, exciting chapter.

Diana wished she could rid herself of her other companion, Mildred, who had proved to be no companion at all and made life at Whitley House so disagreeable. However,

Diana could put her out of her mind for a while at least. The morning after Regina's invitation, Diana left the Clarendon and returned to Whitley House to let the household know she had decided to make a longer stay in town and give them her new direction. Mildred had asked all kinds of probing questions, obviously eaten up with curiosity as to how Diana had made the acquaintance of the daughter of a marquess and been invited to stay with her.

"No doubt you planned this flit to London before my poor brother was even cold in his grave and you intend to find some here-and-therian to install in his place," Mildred said with a disparaging sniff, her arms folded across her bosom.

Association with Lady Regina had given Diana more confidence, so rather than cowering before this attack, Diana merely looked at Mildred in simulated shock and exclaimed: "Such language! I am surprised at you, Mildred."

This admonition startled Mildred so much that she was silenced for a good twenty seconds, during which time Diana bid her goodbye and got back in the carriage to return to London. A little more than an hour later Regina joyfully welcomed her to her home and showed her to a very charming guest room, where Sally unpacked Diana's things. That evening, over dinner, Diana told Regina about her conversation with Mildred.

"I must be a better actress than I thought, to be able to convince her that I was shocked by her use of the term 'here-and-therian.' My father was a sailor, after all, and they're not known for their polite speech," Diana said, chuckling a little at the memory of Mildred's expression.

"Well, while not a particularly shocking one, it *is* a slang term. And she sounds like a very proper lady, so she must have been annoyed with you to have used it. My mother always cautioned me never to use the expressions I picked up from my brother and his friends. It's another of those things that infuriates me that men are allowed to do that we ladies are not," Regina said.

"But you seem not to let such rules bother you in the least. I have noticed that you live alone, with no older female. Surely you defy convention by doing so," Diana said, as this had been a matter of much curiosity to her.

"I am not as courageous as I seem, Diana. It is only recently that I set up an establishment in town. I lived hidden in the country for most of the past ten years, and only came when I thought I was old enough to dispense with a chaperone. Also, I reasoned that I was unlikely to gain society's approval no matter what I did, so I decided to suit my own convenience. However, my outings have been simple ones thus far, where I felt I was unlikely to draw any notice to myself. Even the few times I went to the theatre or opera, I dressed modestly and took a footman for protection. If I had found an older woman who might have proved to be a true companion, I would have had no objection to having her live with me. But now I have *you*. At least for a few weeks, though you're welcome to stay indefinitely," she said, with a warm smile at her friend.

The next day the two ladies met again with the other Ladies of the Registry and wrote out invitations to the ball, which would be held at Lady Gordon's townhome a fortnight hence. Diana, whose knowledge of society gentlemen was virtually nil, allowed the other ladies to determine the guest list, although she willingly helped in the addressing of the invitations. The ladies had not confined those invited to younger sons; Lady Gordon was quite knowledgeable about London society and included other gentlemen, and ladies, whom she thought were good company.

Diana had been startled to see that her name was listed alongside Lady Regina's and Lady Gordon's as a hostess and would have begged to be left off if the others hadn't insisted, thinking they were doing her a great honor and stating, quite truthfully, that without her the ball would not even be taking place.

Diana decided to enter into the spirit of the occasion and resolved to set aside all her doubts and worries. She had never attended a ball, nor danced with a gentleman, though she had learned the steps during those few months she'd attended school. She, who had been married, had never been properly kissed. She was only five-and-twenty, not five-and-eighty, and it was surely past time for her cloistered life to come to an end, and for her to awake from her long slumber.

5

WHEN MAXWELL FIRST received the invitation to the ball, he didn't even open it, and it sat on his mantel for an entire day. He was so sunk in depression that the delicate, feminine handwriting his name and address were written in failed to arouse much curiosity.

It was only later, after he learned *who* had sent it, that he traced the words with an unsteady finger, hardly daring to believe that *she* had written to him.

He had spent the fortnight or so since she'd called on him in a fever of self-castigation and vacillation. That he, a so-called gentleman, should disconcert a lady so! His regret and indecision kept him awake at night. He was finally able to reach the conclusion that he should, at the very least, prevent any more copies of the directory from being sold, but he found when he went to the printer that the only way to accomplish that was to pay an exorbitant sum that he did not possess. Still, he wondered if he should somehow acquire the funds to stop distribution. Surely it behooved him to do so.

His worries were only amplified when he ventured out to dine at his club and chanced to overhear a few men discussing the directory and comparing notes on the ladies they were acquainted with or planned to meet. The discussion finally deteriorated into a squabble, as two of the men insisted that they be given a clear field to the same lady. He winced at talk that would have probably amused him in his former ignorance, and he wondered that he had ever been so blind. His only consolation was that Diana's name was not mentioned during that discussion, or he might have so forgotten himself as to become involved in an altercation.

So it was quite a surprise—nay, a shock—when he finally broke the seal, opened the mysterious invitation, and read:

The company of _Mr. Maxwell Dean_ is requested
at a BALL at No. 46 Berkeley Square
on Thursday, May 29th at 6 p.m.
Hosted by
Lady Regina Townsend,
M. Diana Boyle, Lady Gordon
and the other Ladies of the Registry

Scribbled across the top were the words:

Hope to see you there. — _D. Boyle_

Maxwell read it multiple times, trying to make sense of it. But even after studying it thoroughly he could not surmise what deeper meaning it held. He wanted to believe it meant Mrs. Boyle had forgiven him, but he had done nothing to deserve such a boon, and wondered instead if it could be some elaborate ploy to take revenge on him. But how could an invitation to a ball be an act of revenge? And the very fact that it was being held at Lady Gordon's townhouse and was being hosted by the "Ladies of the Registry" showed that it was no longer Diana alone who was aware of his much-regretted directory, but the other women had also become involved, no doubt at her instigation. The prospect of emigrating to America had never seemed so appealing. But then a sudden image arose in his mind of Diana standing before him in his rooms, those glowing amber eyes raised to his, and he doubted he could bring himself to stay away. It was an opportunity he never thought he'd have, to see her again, perhaps even to dance with her. And even if she were not seeking vengeance she'd have it, because he'd be taunted again with the knowledge of what could never be.

It wasn't that he was in love with her; he knew that he was not. He was not a believer in love at first sight, thinking it only occurred in books or between fools who thought they could judge by appearances. But he had found her very attractive, and she'd had such an air of vulnerability that it had stirred within him a protective desire he'd never felt before. So far was he from wanting to be the source of her distress, he wished he could keep any distress from touching her at all. And knowing that she did not, could not, feel similarly about him made her unattainable and thus somehow more desirable. Though there had been *something* that had passed between them; some instant connection that he was sure she had felt as well. Even the maid couldn't have been unaware of it; so strong a force was it that even the air around them had seemed to vibrate.

He knew it was the height of folly to wish for what one could not have. That had been the reason behind his drawing up his directory in the first place, so that he, and other men, would not waste time and energy longing for what could never be. And yet in a perverse twist of fate, his directory had put him in the very position it had been created to help him avoid.

WHILE THE INVITATION to the ball didn't eliminate Maxwell's anxiety, it did relieve it to some extent. Obviously, as the ladies had made a public espousal of the directory, there was no longer any question of him having to raise funds to halt its distribution. And Mrs. Boyle's brief note demonstrated that she considered herself to be on speaking terms with him, at any rate. So when Lord Jerome invited him to attend a farewell performance by John

Kemble at Covent Garden, he readily agreed, pleased at the prospect of a mindless evening of entertainment with no thoughts of his directory or Mrs. Boyle to torment him.

However, at the intermission, Lord Jerome's first words to him were "Did you happen to receive an invitation to this ball at Lady Gordon's?"

"I did," Maxwell said.

"It appears the ladies are no longer in ignorance of their inclusion in your directory," Lord Jerome said, and Maxwell winced to hear it described as *his*, though Lord Jerome had been aware that Max had authored it all along.

"It appears not. Do you mean to attend the ball?" Max asked.

"I do. In fact, I plan to astound them with my promptitude."

"I'm sure we'll all be astounded," Maxwell replied, as he had watched the first two acts of the play alone before Lord Jerome had finally joined him halfway through the third.

"I wonder how Mrs. Boyle made Lady Regina's acquaintance," Lord Jerome said. "It appears they're fast friends, but I doubt they could have known each other long. And they're hosting this ball together as well."

Mr. Dean was confused by his friend's observation, as it seemed to have come out of nowhere, until he followed Lord Jerome's gaze and saw Mrs. Boyle sitting with another lady, barely twenty feet away.

He could hardly believe that she was real; he felt as if he must have conjured her up from the force of his imaginings. But she was not dressed in unrelieved black as she'd been at their first meeting, and seeing her again in person made him realize what a paltry thing his memories had been. She was even lovelier than he'd imagined her to be.

As if she felt the weight of his stare, she suddenly turned, meeting his eyes directly. He was still grappling with the confusion and excitement generated by her unexpected appearance but retained enough presence of mind to incline his head in greeting. She returned his nod and her lips parted in a slight smile. Then her eyes shifted to take in the other inhabitant of the box before she quickly averted her gaze.

Max realized Jerome had nodded to her as well, though it seemed as if Mrs. Boyle had turned before she'd noticed him. "Are you acquainted with Mrs. Boyle?" Maxwell asked.

Jerome smiled a twisted smile. "Apparently not."

Before Maxwell could pursue this further, the other lady in the box had glanced in their direction. Her eyes passed over Maxwell without recognition, but she appeared startled to see Jerome. She did not nod but after a moment her severe expression relaxed and a hesitant, shy smile appeared. Jerome inclined his head, and her smile widened as she returned his nod.

"Is that Lady Regina Townsend? You're acquainted with her as well?" Max asked his friend.

"I was," Jerome replied. "She's been out of society for many years now."

Maxwell had a vague recollection of some scandal attached to Lady Regina in the past, but not being interested in gossip, he couldn't call it to mind. However, he did remember her name had been linked with Jerome's at some point. "Am I remembering correctly—were you two *engaged*?" he asked, after pulling that tidbit from some dank and dusty corridor of his brain.

"*I* thought so, at any rate," Lord Jerome replied, and Max wished his friend wasn't always so dashed flippant. Jerome must have sensed Maxwell's annoyance because he then said more seriously, "Our parents arranged it when she was fifteen and I was nineteen. She called it off two years later."

Their conversation was interrupted when the curtain rose again on the operatic drama *The Libertine*, a condensed version of Mozart's *Don Giovanni*. Max was sorry it was on the program that evening, however much he might enjoy Mozart. Even though Max knew Don Giovanni would receive the punishment he deserved, he wasn't entirely comfortable watching him play the role of heartless libertine and ravisher of women, knowing Mrs. Boyle was watching as well. It could do nothing to raise her estimation of his sex. He could only hope Don Ottavio's loyalty and love for his fiancée would do a little to offset the villainy of the title character in Mrs. Boyle's mind.

Max was not even aware he was studying Mrs. Boyle with more intensity than he watched the onstage antics until Jerome brought it to his attention. "I begin to wonder why you did not keep your knowledge of such a prize to yourself, instead of announcing her name and direction to the world," he said, his gaze following Maxwell's, at which point Max turned his attention back to the stage. It wouldn't do for Mrs. Boyle to catch them staring at her as if she were a bonbon in a confectionery shop window.

"I hadn't met her until after I published that directory. I've regretted doing it a thousand times since," Maxwell replied.

"But would you have met her if you hadn't published it?" Jerome asked.

"Most likely not."

"Then you shouldn't waste your time on useless regrets," Jerome told him. Maxwell had no reply to this, and they sat silently through a particularly loud duet before Jerome suggested that they visit the ladies' box at the next intermission.

DIANA WAS COMPLETELY overwhelmed. She had never experienced anything like this, her first visit to the theatre, and had never even seen such a large group of persons gathered together in one place. She couldn't venture a guess as to how many were there, but it had to be thousands. She no longer felt like plain, ordinary Diana Boyle, but had entered a fantasy world where she wore expensive jewelry (loaned to her by Lady Regina) and dressed so elegantly she did not even recognize herself when she looked in the mirror.

The fantasy had begun days earlier when Regina had insisted that Diana have a new dress for her first visit to the opera and had taken Diana to her own modiste. Diana had considered her wardrobe more than sufficient, as she had only recently purchased new clothing after putting aside her mourning clothes a few months ago, but it was true that she had very few dresses for evening wear. And it had been such fun to have Regina, who was the most stylish lady Diana had ever seen, to advise her. Though it had been a trifle bittersweet as well, as it made Diana think how much she would have enjoyed treating her mother to a fashionable new wardrobe. Her mother had sacrificed almost every presentable gown she'd owned to remake them for Diana, and it pained Diana to think she would never have the opportunity to repay her mother for all of her sacrifices. However, Diana firmly put those thoughts aside, as she knew Susannah would not want her memory to evoke such sadness. In an effort to cheer herself, Diana looked admiringly down at her new gold lamé gown and shifted in her seat so that she could see once again how it sparkled when it caught the light from the nearby candelabra.

She had enjoyed the play far more than she was enjoying

the opera; she was dismayed by the wickedness of the titular character (as Mr. Dean had foreseen), and so found her mind wandering. She made a concerted effort not to let her *eyes* wander as well, because she was very aware that Mr. Dean's head was frequently turned in her direction, and it was as if she could feel his eyes roaming over her face, so intense was his stare. She did not want him to know she was also affected by his presence and that it took all her self-control not to stare back at him, devastatingly handsome as he was in his evening dress.

His appearance at the theatre had been quite a surprise. She had not thought to see him again until the ball—and there was no guarantee he would even attend—so she had resigned herself to the fact that she might *never* meet him again, and then chided herself for her disappointment at that eventuality. But she couldn't deny the thrill she'd felt when she'd caught sight of him tonight, as if she had unexpectedly run into an old friend. However, seeing Lord Jerome seated next to him had ruined some of her pleasure. It could only remind her that it was because of Mr. Dean that Lord Jerome and Mr. Pryce had called on her in pursuit of her fortune, and that Mr. Dean was little more than a fortune hunter himself.

Her initial surprise at seeing him there was nothing compared to her feelings when he and Lord Jerome walked into her box during the next intermission. She had glanced in their direction a moment before and had noticed the men were gone but assumed they had left the theatre, so she'd been completely taken aback to suddenly find them bowing to her and Regina. Her heart thumped so loudly she could only hope no one else could hear it, and she struggled to get her breathing under control.

Diana hadn't realized that Regina was unacquainted with Mr. Dean. Neither had she previously been aware that Lord Jerome and Lady Regina *did* know each other. Though it seemed to Diana they were uneasy in each other's company, as she watched Lord Jerome greet Lady Regina somewhat stiffly before introducing his companion to her.

"So you're the infamous Mr. Dean," Regina said, after he'd pronounced himself honored to make her acquaintance.

Max glanced at Diana and smiled slightly, almost apologetically, before answering Regina. "My reputation precedes me, I see."

"We are two of a kind, Mr. Dean, as I have a reputation myself," Lady Regina replied, with an enigmatic look at Lord Jerome.

"Not the reputation you deserve," Diana quickly responded, as she couldn't bear to hear Regina denigrate herself. "Lady Regina is the most patient, gracious hostess you could ever imagine," she told the gentlemen, forgetting her shyness in her eagerness to defend her friend. "I am sure she could find a thousand better things to do with her time than escort me around London, but she has kindly done so, and shown great forbearance in the face of my complete lack of sophistication."

The gentlemen, watching Diana as she smiled sweetly at her friend, were both thinking there would be no forbearance required, and that they would gladly take Lady Regina's place as her escort. "Such a loyal friend you have, Lady Regina," Lord Jerome drawled. "I'm glad to hear you value her as you ought."

"So formal, Jerome? I believe we can dispense with titles. You used to call me by my Christian name."

"Very true. However, I was not sure what degree of acquaintance you expected me to claim. Our last correspondence, prior to your recent invitation, taught me not to presume too much."

Despite the dimness of the theatre, it was obvious that Regina blushed at Lord Jerome's words, and she began plying her fan furiously. There was an awkward silence, and Diana wondered if Regina wanted her to somehow rid them of their callers, though she had no idea how to do so. She was grateful when Mr. Dean began speaking; his calm, low tone carried no hidden messages as Lord Jerome's did.

"I am glad you're enjoying your visit, Mrs. Boyle. Have you seen the Elgin Marbles?"

"We have not, though we hope to do so after the ball. It's one of the few sights Lady Regina has not yet seen, so it has the virtue of novelty for both of us," Diana said, looking at Regina with a smile, and she was pleased to see that her friend had regained her usual composure.

"Gentlemen, you must wonder how Mrs. Boyle could praise my skills as a hostess when I have not yet invited you to take a seat. Please do so, if you'd like."

Mr. Dean was quick to move to Mrs. Boyle's side before Lord Jerome could, but Lord Jerome did not display any disappointment and seemed just as happy to take a seat next to Lady Regina. Diana, who had begun to suspect that Lord Jerome might be Regina's former fiancé, hoped Regina was not too disturbed by his attentions. However, Lord Jerome's first words to her were inquiries as to the health of her family, and Diana was pleased to note his voice was not tinged with sarcasm as it frequently was, but that he sounded sincere. Seeing Lady Regina and Lord Jerome conversing easily about people unknown to her, Diana turned her attention to Mr. Dean, wondering if she would have the courage to flirt with him a little, as she'd previously determined to do.

"I was very surprised to receive the invitation to your ball," Mr. Dean said softly, and Diana inched a little closer to him so as not to disturb the other couple's conversation.

"I imagine you were," Diana said, embarrassed, as she did not know how to explain to him her complete reversal from her previous stance.

"I hope it means that you have forgiven me, at least a little, for publishing the directory."

Diana hesitated before replying. Though her initial

anger had faded a great deal, she still thought it was wrong of Mr. Dean to do what he had done, despite it leading to her current, happier situation. She felt it was unconscionable for any person to marry another for their fortune, regardless of their sex, but knew that she was the last person who could say so. Whenever she recalled his question about her motives for her first marriage, she felt the same pang of excruciating embarrassment she had at the time he had asked it.

But seeing him frown at her continued silence, Diana did what she could to reassure him. "You have the forgiveness of most of the ladies, at least. They were not so horrified as I was. Indeed, it was their idea that we embrace the fame the directory has given us."

"But *you* still cannot forgive me?" Mr. Dean asked, and she wondered that it mattered so much to him, as she could see by his expression that it did.

"I didn't say that, exactly. I'm not so angry as I was at first, and I can't deny that its publication has inadvertently had some beneficial effects; it led to my friendship with Lady Regina, for one. But I still find the very notion of such a directory troublesome. And I do wonder why a gentleman would be under the necessity of marrying a fortune when he could acquire one by engaging in a profession, unlike we ladies, who have almost no options at all."

"Gentlemen, too, have fewer options than you might

think. It's no easy task to make a fortune, or it would be a much more common occurrence," Mr. Dean said, with a slight smile.

"But you could go into the military, or the church. I know such professions do not make a man a fortune, but they do provide *some* income."

"I realize we live in an age where it's considered manly to kill one's fellow creatures, whether in war or a duel, but I have a difficult time reconciling my conscience to such a thing. And a gentleman must *purchase* an officer's commission, so it's not a career for the truly impoverished. Nor am I desirous of having a moneymaking sinecure in the church, which is frequently attained through social or family connections and has very little to do with a man's qualifications or even his piety."

Diana stared at him a moment, completely taken aback. She'd never heard any man express such odd opinions. Was he a member of that group—what was it called—the Quakers? But surely he wouldn't be here at the theatre if he were.

"Do you hunt?" she asked.

"On occasion. I'm not as opposed to killing a fox as I am a human, though it does seem strange that we have glorified the process of doing so. Do *you* hunt?"

"No, but not because I have a strong ethical objection to it. It's just—I've never learned to ride," Diana said. She imagined such a confession would immediately make obvious to Mr. Dean the lowness of her origins. However, his admiring expression did not change.

"Would you like to?" he asked.

"Are you offering to teach me?" The question did not come out coquettishly as Diana had intended but almost as if she were issuing a challenge. She couldn't seem to get the knack of this flirting business.

"I am. I would do much to overcome your initial poor impression of me. Though if you spend too much time in my company it might have the opposite effect," Mr. Dean said, with a self-deprecating smile.

Diana smiled back. "Oh, I don't know. We've been able to converse quite amiably for all of five minutes. Who knows how far our relationship could progress at our next meeting," she said, and then wished she could withdraw her last sentence. It sounded less like flirtation and more like an invitation. The poor man's head must be spinning at how she switched from cold to hot and back again. However, though a glint in his eyes betrayed an awareness of her words, he was too gentlemanly to embarrass her.

"I hope it will at least progress to the point that we might dance together. May I claim two dances at your ball? The supper dance, perhaps? And a waltz?"

Diana shyly acquiesced, and as Lady Regina and Lord Jerome had reached a lull in their conversation and had overheard Mr. Dean's question, Lord Jerome also requested a dance from Lady Regina and Diana, and Mr. Dean likewise asked one of Lady Regina.

The intermission ended shortly thereafter, and the gentlemen took their leave of the ladies, assuring them they would see them next week at the ball.

When they were back in their own box, Maxwell turned to Lord Jerome, asking him how he'd made Mrs. Boyle's acquaintance.

"I called on her at her home in Twickenham," Jerome replied.

"So it was you," Max said, rather enigmatically.

"What is that supposed to mean?" Jerome asked, ignoring the drama onstage in favor of their discussion, even though he usually disliked conversation during a performance.

"She complained to me that, because of my directory, gentlemen unknown to her had called at her home, angling for a dinner invitation," Max replied.

"Well, it wasn't *just* me. That idiot Pryce was there as well, and I wasn't exactly thrilled to be thrown into his company myself. I suspect he's the one who gave the whole game away. She certainly didn't learn about it from me." Jerome watched the opera for a moment before turning back to his friend in exasperation. "You have some nerve complaining that I called upon Mrs. Boyle. What did you expect me to do when you made me a present of that blasted directory? I thought by choosing someone unknown to society I'd at least be sparing myself a reputation as a fortune hunter."

"I told you; I regret the entire thing. I should never

have done it. She doesn't want a bunch of strange men paying court to her."

"I resent that description, although I assume you mean 'strange' in the sense that we're unknown to her," Jerome said. "It seems that she has changed her mind, however, or why else would she be throwing this ball?"

Max shrugged. "I get the impression the other ladies suggested it. It doesn't seem as if *they* mind the attention."

"Lady Regina certainly does not. Gives her an excuse to rejoin society after all these years."

Max eyed his friend curiously. Jerome didn't give away much, but it seemed to Max he displayed a lingering bitterness toward Lady Regina. "Do you still have an interest there?" he asked Jerome.

"I'd be a fool if I did. Oh, I was fond of her during our betrothal, but she was still little more than a child. I was waiting for her to grow up. And then she did, and decided she had no interest in *me*. And it's entirely owing to her jilting of me that I'm now forced to look around for a wife I'm not even sure I want."

"But you wouldn't have minded being married to Lady Regina?" Max asked.

"I was fond of her, like I said. And our families were close, though that changed after she ended the betrothal. Before that, everything was wrapped up very nicely. My future was assured. And then—" He stopped suddenly, as if conscious that he was about to divulge too much.

"She was involved in some scandal?" Maxwell prompted him.

Jerome hesitated, then nodded. "I wasn't going to tell you; I still feel this urge to protect her, probably since we were affianced for two years. But since it's common knowledge I suppose it can do no harm for you to know. She eloped. Her father tracked her down before she made it to Gretna Green with the man, but not in time to prevent her from losing her reputation."

"And he didn't marry her?" Maxwell asked, shocked.

"I was never apprised of the exact details, but it appears *she* no longer wanted to marry *him*."

"Poor girl," Max said sympathetically. "I hope she wasn't mistreated in any way. How old did you say she was?"

"She was seventeen," Jerome said, darting a quick glance at Lady Regina, his brow furrowed. "I hadn't ever really thought, I mean, I just assumed—" he said, in an uncertain tone Max had never heard him use before. "Do you think I should have called the scoundrel out? But she had already jilted me, surely her father would have taken action if it was necessary?"

"You know my opinion of dueling. A bout of fisticuffs, on the other hand . . ." Maxwell said, his voice trailing off suggestively.

"Yes, that would have been very satisfying. I'm sorry I didn't think of it at the time," Jerome said, a little absently.

He was still staring at Lady Regina with a frown, as if reconsidering his view of their past history.

Maxwell, turning his attention back to the stage in time to see the villainous Don Giovanni descend into the flames of hell, reflected that it was no more than some men deserved.

6

Diana had very little confidence in her dancing ability, as it had been many years since she'd had lessons, and Regina had been out of society for so long that she was out of practice as well, so the two women decided to engage a dancing master to come every day in the ten days leading up to the ball.

They felt a little sorry for their instructor, Monsieur de la Tour, as he was a French émigré who had fled the revolution almost twenty-five years earlier at the tender age of sixteen and had eventually begun giving dance lessons as a way of putting food on the table. Though Diana supposed, as professions went, his wasn't an unpleasant one. After her conversation with Mr. Dean, she'd been forced to acknowledge to herself that he was probably correct in saying it was no easy matter for a gentleman to earn an income, though she still contended that an impoverished lady had it far worse.

After a private discussion, Regina and Diana hit upon the notion of inviting Monsieur de la Tour to their ball. Although forty years old, he was a bachelor, and was certainly as deserving of an advantageous marriage as the younger son of an Englishman, as he had lost his fortune and property in France through no fault of his own. He was also a very personable man, with his dark hair and eyes, athletic grace, and Gallic charm. However, he appeared more startled than pleased by the invitation.

"I do not understand. You wish to engage me to work for the evening?" he asked them, puzzled. "You want me to be on hand to remind you of the steps should you forget?"

"Although of course we'd appreciate any reminders you think necessary, we're inviting you as our guest," Lady Regina said, still slightly red-cheeked and perspiring from the quadrille she had just finished, where she had obligingly performed the man's part opposite Diana so Monsieur could watch them both.

"But it is quite scandalous to invite someone such as me to a society ball," he protested.

Diana and Regina smiled at each other. "Most likely the ball itself will cause a scandal," Diana said. "It is no matter, though, because we do not care."

"*C'est incroyable!*" he exclaimed. "The English are always guarding their females from us poor dancing masters. They'd sooner invite the fox into the chicken . . . What is the word?"

"Coop," said Diana and Regina simultaneously, and then smiled when Monsieur de la Tour repeated the word with his French-accented English.

Monsieur smiled as well, before sweeping them an elaborate bow. "I thank you, ladies, for the invitation; I am honored to accept. I have never before danced with any of my students for pleasure, though I take what pleasure I can in the performance of my duties," he said, with a flirtatious glance at Regina. "I greatly look forward to dancing at your ball. Might I request a dance with each of you?"

The ladies happily agreed, Diana mentioning later to Regina that it was an inspired idea to invite Monsieur de la Tour, as there would be no other gentleman there who danced so well, and they would both feel much more confident with him as a partner.

"And perhaps one of the ladies will fall in love with him, and have a dancing partner for life," Regina said, with a laugh.

Diana, who had noticed her friend seemed to take a great deal of pleasure in her dancing lessons, most particularly when the instruction involved *waltzing* with Monsieur de la Tour, wondered if Regina herself might be developing a fondness for the gentleman. And if she were, Diana thought it was a fortunate thing she could afford to marry him.

THE LADIES OF the Registry met at Lady Gordon's town-home to make the final arrangements for their ball. There were now eighteen members of their group, and Diana felt they were the best of the bunch, as they did not look down their noses at Lady Regina because of her lost reputation, or sneer at Miss Jarmyn, whose fortune had been acquired from her grandfather, a Yorkshire millowner. They were also fully aware that their participation could cost them vouchers to Almack's Assembly Rooms or invitations to Carlton House, and they were willing to make that sacrifice.

Even Diana, as removed from society as she was, had heard of Almack's. Dances were held there every Wednesday evening during the season and were by invitation only. To be given vouchers to Almack's was the ultimate sign of social acceptance. While noble birth was an important consideration, it did not guarantee entry, nor were all those of inferior birth denied admittance. After all, Beau Brummel, the famous dandy, was a frequent attendee, and his grandfather had been a servant and his father a shop-keeper. Whether or not someone received a voucher was entirely due to the whims of a small group of seven women: the Lady Patronesses of Almack's. These patronesses also required young ladies who had never yet danced the waltz in public to approach them for permission before doing so. To circumvent the patronesses' authority and start a rival group could cause the Ladies of the Registry to be ostracized by their peers, who courted the favor of the powerful and prestigious patronesses. But Diana and the other ladies were not in fear of society's disapproval. On the contrary, they felt they had played by its rules long enough or, as in Diana's case, did not aspire to a position in such exalted circles. Somehow the very thing that had been the symbol of their helplessness, that directory which listed them as no more than a commodity, had now become a way for them to exert their independence, to rewrite the rules in their favor.

And they were quite literally rewriting them.

Lady Regina, seated at a desk in Lady Gordon's library, spoke aloud as she scribbled on a sheet of paper.

"Number one: Any lady may refuse to dance with a gentleman and still have the option of dancing with another gentleman should she wish to," she said slowly, squinting down at the sentence she'd written and nodding in satisfaction. She then looked up at the ladies who were seated around her and who were staring at her with expressions of shock and confusion. "Was that unclear?" Regina asked them.

"But . . . do you mean we can refuse *any* gentleman? And we don't have to sit out the remainder of the dances?" asked Miss Meadows.

Regina looked back down at her paper. "Isn't that what I've written? Should I phrase it differently?"

Lady Gordon intervened. "I believe, Lady Regina, that

Miss Meadows, and some of the other ladies, are asking about the suitability of the rule, not its clarity."

"Ah," Lady Regina said. "Perhaps we should discuss it then. I realize that it's considered impolite to refuse a gentleman's offer to dance, and if a lady does so she's required to sit out the rest of the dances that evening, but I believe that rule to be arbitrary, and well, stupid, and quite obviously designed for a man's benefit, and not a woman's."

"I agree," Lady Gordon said, nodding her head emphatically. "A woman should not be forced to participate in any activity with a gentleman if she does not desire to, and she should not be punished for exercising that right."

Most of the ladies began nodding in agreement, though a few still looked uncertain.

"But what do we say?" Mrs. Young asked. She had been sought after even prior to her inclusion in the directory, as she was pretty and good-natured, and the late Mr. Young had been popular before his untimely death. "In the past, if I did not want to dance with a gentleman, I merely told him that I was not dancing that evening."

"That is a very good question," Lady Regina said. "Any suggestions?"

"We would still have to be polite. There is no sense in needlessly causing offense, or hurting some poor gentleman's feelings," Diana said, as she was very softhearted and could imagine how humiliating it would be for a shy young gentleman to be brusquely refused after having gathered his courage to approach a lady and request a dance.

"Perhaps it should be the ladies who ask the gentlemen to dance," Miss Jarmyn said, and even Lady Regina looked a little surprised at this suggestion.

"What do you think?" Lady Regina asked Lady Gordon.

Lady Gordon addressed the group. "I think that if any of you ladies desire to dance with a gentleman who has not asked you, then you should inform one of the hostesses: me, Lady Regina, or Mrs. Boyle, and we will present you to the gentleman as a desirable partner."

"And if you do not want to dance with a gentleman, you can merely say, 'I thank you very much for the invitation, but I beg you to excuse me,'" suggested Lady Regina. "Hopefully there will not be so many undesirable gentlemen present that you need refuse them."

The ladies nodded agreement to this, some of them looking quite relieved, and Diana doubted very many, if any, gentlemen would be refused, if merely the thought of such a prospect made the ladies this uncomfortable.

Regina had turned her attention back to her document and the only sound in the room was the scratching of her pen, as the ladies waited in silent anticipation. "Number two: A lady may dance with the same gentleman more than two times," she read aloud, before adding: "should she so desire," as she wrote down those words. There were little gasps around the room, but when Regina looked up, the expressions were pleased.

"Any questions or objections?" Regina asked.

"Exactly how many times *may* they dance together?" Miss Meadows asked.

"Why, I don't know," Regina said. "What do you ladies think?"

"Perhaps we shouldn't impose a limit," said Miss Jarmyn, who was beginning to appear quite the rebel.

"We could leave it up to each lady's own discretion," Diana said, "but we should keep in mind that a certain amount of restraint is usually advisable."

"We wouldn't want the gentleman to be *too* sure of himself," Miss Ballard agreed.

The final rule the group decided upon was that any lady present at the ball was allowed to waltz.

"There is no point in waiting to get permission from the patronesses of Almack's, as very few, if any of us, plan to attend their boring assemblies," Regina explained. She didn't add that they were unlikely to be invited anyway, once news of this scandalous ball had spread. This rule was unanimously and happily adopted, and shortly thereafter most of the ladies took their leave, although Regina and Diana stayed behind to finalize many other more mundane details with Lady Gordon.

Diana, who had never hosted a social event larger than an informal dinner, was thankful that they had Lady Gordon to guide them. Even Lady Regina, whose knowledge of such things was obviously greater than Diana's, had never planned and hosted her own ball, though she had seen her mother do so.

Lady Gordon had been a widow for five years, but her husband had been quite active in political affairs before his death, so she was accustomed to entertaining and enjoyed doing so. She confided in Diana and Lady Regina that her marriage had been a happy one, and her one regret was that she and her husband had had no children. Upon his death his title and country home had gone to a distant relation, but his fortune had been his to bestow, and Lady Gordon had inherited most of it, along with the town-house in Berkeley Square.

"I very much doubt I shall ever remarry," she told Regina and Diana during their tour of the ballroom, as she looked around in fond reminiscence. "It was a huge surprise when I found I was included in this directory. Mr. Dean must not have realized I am two-and-forty. And while I greatly miss my husband, I realize I was more fortunate than most women to have fifteen years of happiness with a man who returned my affection, and who sought and valued my opinion. It would be very difficult to find another man like him, and I'd feel silly searching for one at my age."

"You were fortunate, indeed," Diana said emphatically, and then wished she had not spoken, as the other two ladies looked curiously at her. She hurried to change the subject. "Though I agree it would be difficult to find another gentleman worthy of you," she said, with a fond smile at Lady Gordon.

"I'm sure most of the gentlemen are looking for a younger woman, with whom they can start a family," said Lady Gordon with a momentary frown, before resuming her usual pleasant expression. "But my goal in doing this is not to find myself a husband, but to participate in Lady Regina's very revolutionary and novel scheme to remake the typical gender roles in our favor. And, though I know one of the rules you probably intend to flout is that young, unmarried ladies must have an older female chaperone, I figured it wouldn't hurt to have someone of the sort to lend respectability to your endeavor."

"We greatly appreciate your doing so, Lady Gordon," Regina told her. "Indeed, I don't know if I'd be brave enough to undertake this at all without your support."

The discussion then turned to some of the practical decisions to be made regarding the menu, and while Lady Gordon and Regina debated the merits of serving Punch à la Romaine, Diana studied their hostess.

Lady Gordon could obviously no longer pass for a debutante, but she was still a very lovely woman. It was her hair that proclaimed her age, as it had turned completely gray, but rather than detract from her appearance, the color seemed to emphasize her lustrous eyes, which were the color of an aquamarine gemstone. Her figure, too, was very pleasing and her movements graceful, and Diana suspected that some men might prefer her elegant maturity to less-polished youthfulness.

Now that she had gotten to know some of the other women, Diana felt much less apprehensive and was growing more excited about the upcoming ball. Although many of these women had been born into far more affluent circumstances than she had, they had all experienced the restrictions brought on by virtue of their sex, and now they were getting the opportunity to taste some of the freedoms that a gentleman took for granted. Of course, they were all very little things; so trifling that a man would probably find them ridiculous. But having been trapped in a gilded cage, even a short flight was better than never once being allowed to spread one's wings.

7

REGINA WALKED INTO Diana's room just as Sally was putting a jeweled comb into her mistress's hair, atop an elaborate arrangement of braids and curls. Diana was careful not to move until Sally had finished, and Regina waited patiently to speak until after the maid stepped back and Diana had gotten up from her seat at the vanity to turn and face Regina.

"Oh, Diana, you're an absolute vision! No one will even look my way with you nearby," Regina said, but in an affectionate tone that made it obvious she was not truly envious of her friend.

"Even if that were true, you have only yourself to blame," Diana said in a teasing tone of voice. "I would not be looking so fashionable without your expert guidance." The two ladies smiled at each other in genuine delight, and Diana had a moment to take in her friend's appearance. "But it's completely untrue that no one will look your way. You are radiant this evening."

Regina sparkled from the diamond and sapphire tiara she wore on her head, to the shiny satin slippers on her feet. But nothing shone so brightly as her eyes, which rivaled the sapphires in brilliance. They were even more lustrous at that moment, filled as they were with moisture that she quickly blinked away.

"Diana, I am so grateful to you. I would never have had the courage to venture into London society again without you by my side," Regina said, pressing Diana's hand between both of her own.

"And if it weren't for you, I would be rusticating at Whitley House right now, tiptoeing around my butler and being scolded by my sister-in-law," Diana replied, and Sally, who was all too familiar with Godfrey and Mildred, gave a small snort of laughter and broke the serious mood.

Reminded of her presence, Diana turned to smile at her maid. "Thank you, Sally, for dressing my hair so well. Shall we go?" she asked Regina, gathering her gloves, reticule, and fan.

A short time later, as she stood at the entrance of Lady Gordon's ballroom at the end of the reception line, Diana could not believe this was all really happening. There had to be a hundred wax candles burning, their light reflected by dozens of mirrors, and Diana thought back to how she and her mother could not afford even one candle made of wax and had made do with tallow ones that stunk of beef and pig fat. She wished so much that her mother could have been there, but was distracted from her poignant reflections when Lady Gordon turned to her and Regina with a smile and asked: "Are you ready to greet our guests?"

Diana felt her stomach cramp from fear; she had never felt so *un*-ready, but Regina squeezed her hand and the two women smiled back at Lady Gordon and nodded. Lady Gordon then spoke to her butler, and he began ushering people into the room.

The other Ladies of the Registry were the first guests to arrive, and Diana's nervousness dissipated a little after exchanging greetings with those already known to her. And then Monsieur de la Tour arrived, whom Regina and Diana introduced to Lady Gordon with proprietary pleasure. He was one of the few persons invited whom Lady Gordon had never met and, though Diana knew he probably didn't have the money for a fashionable tailor, he wore his evening dress with a typical French flair for elegance and was one of the best-looking men in the room. Diana was smiling up at him and reminding him of the dance he'd reserved, when she heard Mr. Dean announced and turned abruptly away. Monsieur de la Tour looked to see who had caused this reaction before continuing into the ballroom, his departure unnoticed by Diana.

"Mr. Dean," Lady Gordon was saying, as he bowed to her. "I am not sure whether to greet you with a smile or a frown." However, Diana was relieved to see—though she couldn't understand why it mattered to her—that Lady Gordon had a very gracious smile on her lips.

"I'm sure I deserve to be frowned at, Lady Gordon. However, your beauty is only enhanced by your smile, so I'm pleased to be the recipient of it," Mr. Dean replied.

Lady Gordon smiled more widely and tapped his shoulder with her fan. "It is fortunate for you that Lady Regina thought of a way to turn your outrageous act to our advantage, or a frown would be the least of what you deserved."

"I am very aware of my good fortune," Mr. Dean said, and Lady Gordon turned to greet the next guest as Mr. Dean bowed to Regina, telling her, "Lady Regina, it is a pleasure to see you again."

And then it was Diana's turn to greet him and his ability to exchange easy chitchat seemed to vanish at the sight of her. "Mr. Dean," Diana said.

"Mrs. Boyle." His eyes flitted quickly over her dress before returning to her face. "You are . . . breathtaking this evening." Since he appeared to be struggling to catch his breath, Diana did not think he was merely flattering her.

"Thank you," Diana replied, and that was the extent of their conversation as the next guest was at his elbow and he was forced to move on.

One of the most surprising arrivals, in Diana's view, was Lady Jersey, a patroness of Almack's and leader of London fashionable society, who was ironically called

"Silence" as she never stopped talking. She demonstrated the appropriateness of her nickname as she held up the line while speaking with Lady Gordon.

"Thank you so much for inviting me to your ball; even though I had to beg for an invitation and it was so *arduous* and lengthy a journey," she said, laughing, as she also lived in Berkeley Square.

"Just do not become offended if our ball does not conform to the rules of the assemblies you host at Almack's," Lady Gordon warned her.

"My dear Lady Gordon, you know that I am not half so formal as the other patronesses. Though it is true I was forced to turn the Duke of Wellington away at the door the other evening. It was seven minutes after eleven. *Seven!* Had he arrived just a few minutes earlier I might have made an exception, but there were so many people watching I felt it would set a dangerous precedent to allow it. However, you are wise not to impose such stringent requirements at *your* little affair," she said, and Diana saw Regina stiffen at the condescending way Lady Jersey referred to their ball. Still, Diana imagined one of the richest women in England wasn't as easily impressed as poor little Diana Boyle, raised in a cottage in Plymouth.

After Lady Jersey's arrival the receiving line broke up, though Regina still appeared to be looking over her shoulder for someone.

"I'm surprised Lord Jerome isn't yet here," she said to Diana, but no sooner had the words left her mouth then he entered and stood just inside the door, scanning the room until his eyes came to rest upon Lady Regina. He bowed in her direction, and she and Diana nodded to him in acknowledgment.

"It's a good thing Lady Jersey isn't manning the door at *our* ball, or Lord Jerome might have been turned away," Diana whispered to her friend, who laughed a little too loudly at the joke, and Diana realized that Lord Jerome still made Regina feel ill at ease. Regina had confided to Diana after they saw Jerome at the theatre that he was her former betrothed and that she was happy she'd conversed with him that evening, as it meant there would be no further constraint between them, but Diana thought Regina had been overly optimistic. There was definitely *something* between Regina and Lord Jerome, though perhaps "constraint" wasn't the correct word for it. And it didn't appear to be going away.

Lord Jerome approached the two women, greeting them and reminding them of the dances he'd reserved, before walking over to join Maxwell.

"I thought you were going to amaze the ladies with your promptitude," Max said.

"This *is* prompt," Lord Jerome drawled. "It's not even eight o'clock."

"The ball started at six," his friend reminded him.

"And what did I miss?"

"You weren't here to greet the ladies."

"In other words, I missed waiting in a line," Jerome

said, and Maxwell couldn't help smiling. "They've out-done themselves," Jerome continued, but Maxwell wasn't sure if he was referring to the sumptuousness of the ball or the ladies' appearances, as his gaze had settled on them once again.

"Do you intend to dance with any ladies other than our hostesses?" Max asked. "There are a number of other ami-able ladies present, and our purpose in coming was to meet them, was it not?"

"Was it?" Jerome asked.

There was a pause, and then Max said, "No, it wasn't." And he joined his friend in gazing at the two women who were the real reason for their presence.

As they watched, a distinguished dark-haired gentle-man approached the ladies and seemed to be on good terms with both, as the group conversed easily and smiled frequently. When the music began the mysterious man led Mrs. Boyle to join a set, and Maxwell watched as they danced together more harmoniously and gracefully than any couple he'd ever seen.

"Who is that?" he asked Jerome.

"I have no idea," Jerome said.

The two men were still watching the dancing when Lady Gordon suddenly appeared before them with a lady on each side, and they were forced to give her their at-tention.

"Lord Jerome, Mr. Dean. May I present Miss Jarmyn to

you both? I believe you are already acquainted with Mrs. Young."

The gentlemen bowed, the ladies curtsied, and Jerome and Max did their obvious duty and asked the ladies to dance.

Maxwell, who had believed his dancing skills to be perfectly adequate before he'd seen Diana dancing with that other gentleman, was now very glad to have a chance to practice before his dance with her. His partner, Miss Jarmyn, seemed agreeable, if a little unconventional.

"Why is Lord Jerome a 'lord' if he's a younger son, and you're a mister?" she asked him, after they'd dispensed with more traditional conversation about the heat of the rooms and her county of origin.

"He's the younger son of a marquis, and unfortunately I'm merely the younger son of a baron," Max said, in a self-mocking tone that he assumed made it obvious he was joking.

"My condolences" was her response.

Max was thankful that the dance ended at that point and he was spared having to reply. He bowed to his partner, and they were walking off the floor together when she surprised him further by saying, "I'll dance with Lord Jerome now."

"I believe he's already engaged for this dance," Max said, a little taken aback. He quickly scanned the room, saw Mr. Pryce watching the dancers, and led his farouche young partner in that direction. "Perhaps I can introduce you to a different gentleman," he offered, and Miss Jarmyn happily agreed. They reached Pryce and Max presented the young lady to him.

"Pleasure to meet you. Is Jarmyn spelled with a *J* or a *G*?" Mr. Pryce asked her, and Maxwell heard her spelling out her name as Pryce escorted her to the dance floor.

It was finally time for the waltz Maxwell had reserved with Mrs. Boyle, and he eagerly started walking toward her when he saw her looking around the room as if in search of someone. He assumed it was him she was looking for, and he smiled in anticipation of meeting her gaze, but her glance passed quickly over him before she apparently found her quarry and hurried to his side: it was the distinguished gentleman she'd danced with for the first set.

He stopped, unsure whether to follow her. Was this why she had insisted he come, so that she could spurn him in favor of another gentleman? It was a very effective revenge, if so, because he felt a pang each time she smiled up at the man, seeming much happier and more carefree than she ever had in Maxwell's presence. But as he watched, he saw Mrs. Boyle lead the man to Lady Gordon, apparently presenting him to *her* as a partner. Expelling a breath of relief, he walked over to join them.

As he approached, he overheard Lady Gordon protesting that she hadn't intended to dance, that she was the hostess.

"I'm also a hostess, and yet I intend to dance most of the evening," Diana told her, turning to smile at Maxwell, who had reached her side. "In fact, here is my next partner now."

Lady Gordon made a little gesture of defeat, before placing her hand on the arm her prospective partner had gracefully extended. "I saw you dancing with Mrs. Boyle and Lady Regina earlier, Monsieur de la Tour, and envied them their partner. I would be pleased to have this opportunity to dance with you."

"Believe me when I say, as trite as it may sound, that the pleasure is mine," Monsieur de la Tour replied, before leading Lady Gordon to the floor.

It seemed to Diana that Lady Gordon, with her erect figure, delicate features, and silver hair, was reminiscent of a noblewoman from the previous century, and that she made a very fitting partner for the elegant Frenchman. Mr. Dean apparently agreed. "They seem well matched," he told Diana, watching the other couple take the floor before turning to Diana and offering her his hand.

This would be Diana's first time waltzing with any man other than her dancing master, and Mr. Dean was the only man she felt inclined to grant that honor. She was grateful he had reserved this dance in advance because she had been able to refuse other requests without having to make any awkward excuses.

She was very conscious of Mr. Dean's hand holding hers, and when they reached the floor and he put his arms around her, she wondered how she had thought herself brave enough to waltz with *any* gentleman. Her husband had never embraced her publicly like this and had only rarely been this close to her in private. But she didn't want to think of Mr. Boyle when Mr. Dean held her in his arms.

"I cannot claim to be as good a dancer as Monsieur de la Tour," he said apologetically.

Diana laughed softly in response, as if he'd made a joke. "I would never hold you to such a high standard," she said with a wide smile, and Mr. Dean frowned, wondering what she could mean. Was it because she esteemed the other man so highly that Max could never hope to compare? He was relieved when she went on to explain: "Monsieur de la Tour makes his living by giving instruction in dance. He has been teaching me and Lady Regina."

It was Maxwell's turn to smile, and his smile was so charming and had such an unsettling effect on Diana that she was forced to look away momentarily to gather her composure.

"I had never even considered such a profession when thinking of those available to gentlemen. I imagine it's preferable to one in the military or the church," he said.

"Perhaps, but I can't help pitying the poor wife of such a man. Imagine her dismay at the thought of her husband holding so many other women in his arms," Diana said, half joking. They danced in silence for a moment, before she said: "I begin to understand why some object to the waltz. It's so very intimate." She then blushed at her unthinking words.

"A person should be very discriminating in their choice of partner, to be sure," Mr. Dean said softly. "I think myself very clever to have secured such a desirable one."

Monsieur de la Tour had forbidden Diana to look down during her dances, so she had no choice but to continue to gaze into Mr. Dean's slate-blue eyes. As he whirled her around the glittering ballroom, she told herself it was the dance that was making her so dizzy and breathless. She hoped Mr. Dean did not think her rude, but she couldn't bring herself to make conversation, as she very much wanted to concentrate on the strange and novel sensations she was feeling; a pleasurable tingling and excitement that she'd only ever experienced in his presence. She could not even find a way to describe it and decided to stop trying to do so and give herself over to experiencing it. Mr. Dean had become silent as well, though his gaze had dropped once from her eyes to her lips, and he had pulled her a little more firmly against him during one of the turns. Or had she moved closer to him? Their legs were most definitely brushing now, and Diana pulled back a little. She had never danced this close to Monsieur de la Tour, and she was sure everyone would notice and be scandalized.

"I beg your pardon," Mr. Dean said huskily, after she had pulled away. "I told you I was not a skilled dancer."

So he *had* pulled her closer. And Diana did not think it

had been unintentional. "I have no complaints," she said. Mr. Dean looked pleasantly surprised at her reply, and the hand at her back shifted a little in what felt like a caress.

Unfortunately, in Diana's view, the dance could not last forever. It seemed to speed by far more quickly than her previous ones, and much too soon Mr. Dean was leading her from the floor.

"Thank you, Mrs. Boyle. I have never enjoyed a dance more. Are there any other waltzes tonight?" he asked hopefully.

"Just one, but I've already promised it to Monsieur de la Tour."

"We've already agreed he's the best dancer here, and you have the pleasure of dancing with him frequently. Surely it would be selfish of you not to allow the other ladies an opportunity to dance with him?" he asked, with a twinkle in his eye.

"I had not thought of it that way. I would not want to be selfish," Diana said, smiling mischievously. "I'll ask him if he would be agreeable to exchanging it for another."

WHILE DIANA WALTZED with Mr. Dean, Lord Jerome was causing similar tumultuous feelings in Lady Regina's breast. This was the romance and excitement she'd longed for when she'd eloped at seventeen, and it struck her as extremely ironic that in trying to rush the experience, she'd instead delayed it by eleven years.

"It's funny to think that we were engaged for two years, and yet this is the first time we've danced together," Lady Regina said.

"Why, so it is," Lord Jerome replied, surprised. They danced in silence for a moment, before he said in a low tone that contained no trace of the sarcasm he was known for: "It was foolish of us to wait so long."

"Perhaps we can make up for lost time. We must dance together at every opportunity," Regina said teasingly, but Jerome did not smile.

"A delightful prospect, indeed," he said, and Regina was sure she saw the admiration she'd hoped to inspire in him so many years ago finally reflected in his eyes.

8

THE BALL HAD been a smashing success. Thanks to Lady Gordon's assistance, the gentlemen who had attended were not vulgar fortune hunters, though most would benefit from an advantageous marriage. Using her familiarity with society, Lady Gordon had invited those gentlemen she knew to be presentable, mannerly, and genteel. (Mr. Pryce was an exception, as his manners were not universally pleasing, but Lady Gordon had predicted, quite rightly, that he would prove amusing. And since he was connected to practically every noble family listed in *Debrett's*, it had done no harm to invite him for that reason, as well.) Each of the gentlemen, realizing they had been one of a select few, were happy to be chosen and even happier to dance attendance on a unique, refreshing group of young women.

After the ball, the Ladies of the Registry, instead of

finding themselves ostracized by those who made up London society, were embraced by them. For it's an indisputable fact that when a woman no longer seeks acceptance, she suddenly becomes irresistible.

Another surprising result of their ball was that Monsieur de la Tour was enjoying as much popularity as the ladies were. Not only was he receiving invitations to numerous society affairs, but he had also been granted an elusive voucher to Almack's. This was due in large part to Lady Jersey having waltzed with him after he had been released by Diana from their dance.

"It seems an unnecessary expense," Monsieur de la Tour told the ladies, speaking of the voucher, "so I doubt I will use it."

"Let me pay for it. I would be glad to," Regina said.

"I appreciate the kind offer, but it has never been an ambition of mine to join high society. They are a capricious bunch. Besides, I already have the opportunity to dance with the loveliest women in London," he said, with a bow to Lady Regina and Diana.

"It would probably be a very effective advertisement for your services," Regina said.

"True. After your ball I acquired three new students."

"That's wonderful! Was Lady Gordon one of them?" Diana asked.

Diana thought it very interesting that the suave and confident Frenchman grew self-conscious at the mere mention of the lady's name. "No, of course not. Lady Gordon has no need of dancing lessons. She is already a very accomplished dancer. It would be a futile exercise for me to cultivate her acquaintance, in more ways than one."

Diana, who had assumed she'd done Monsieur a favor by presenting him to Lady Gordon, now wondered if she'd done him an injury. She had thought her two friends well suited to each other, and she knew Lady Gordon to be lonely and suspected Monsieur de la Tour was as well. But while Diana cared nothing for rank or social status, Lady Gordon might think very differently. Her first husband had been an important figure in political circles and a nobleman. Monsieur de la Tour might be correct in thinking Lady Gordon would never consider a poor dancing master as a second husband, if that's what he meant by saying any further association with her would be futile. And from the tone of his voice when he said it, Diana suspected that *was* his meaning.

THE LADIES OF the Registry had met a few days after the ball to rehash that glorious evening and recount their experiences, and soon formed the habit of meeting regularly either at Lady Gordon's or Lady Regina's home. They frequently encountered one another at social events around town as well. And they had decided to host another evening event together, although not a private ball. This time they planned an excursion to Vauxhall Gardens, and each lady was to choose one gentleman to invite as her escort. And while it was not uncommon for a gentleman to escort a lady to an evening's entertainment, it was unusual for an unmarried lady to be the one extending the invitation.

Mr. Pryce was calling on Miss Jarmyn, and she was apparently quite infatuated with her boyish-looking suitor, his oversized ears notwithstanding. Lady Gordon had told Diana and Regina in private that with Mr. Pryce's tendency to use slang from a lower class of society, Miss Jarmyn might be the only young lady who could understand him. She then apologized for the unkind remark, but Diana and Regina assured her they wouldn't repeat it and agreed that Miss Jarmyn and Mr. Pryce were uniquely suited to each other.

"Perhaps Miss Jarmyn will even teach him some new jargon," Lady Regina said, laughing.

The other ladies hadn't as quickly made up their minds among their various suitors but were enjoying the attention, and their regular meetings slowly changed in focus from social planning to involvement in the charitable institutions that Lady Gordon promoted. Diana knew what it was like to be a penniless young woman with few options, but she also realized her mother had protected her from a far worse fate, and so was determined to do what she could to help other poor women. She and Regina were happy to offer donations and other assistance to a home that Lady Gordon had established for some of these unfortunate women and their children.

Diana also found that she and Lady Gordon shared a

similar regret: they had both hoped for children and had been denied that wish. Diana had not regretted this while she was married to Mr. Boyle; she had been extremely relieved that he seemed disinterested in the marital duties that her mother had explained resulted in a child. But when Diana later decided she would never marry again, she'd felt a sense of loss at the realization that if she gave up matrimony, she was also giving up motherhood. She and Lady Gordon spoke of it when they were alone together in Lady Regina's drawing room one morning, and Lady Gordon confided in Diana that she had even considered bringing one of the orphans home with her.

"I am not sure what the present Lord Gordon would do, however. Have me declared mad and strip me of my fortune, I suppose," Lady Gordon said half-jokingly, though Diana could tell it was something that she cared about deeply.

"I have thought about adopting a child as well," Diana told Lady Gordon. "I have no one to leave Whitley House to after my death, and I would dearly love to help a child in difficult circumstances."

"But, my dear," Lady Gordon said in surprise, "you're so young. You still have plenty of time to start a family. And your husband was much older than you, was he not? If you marry a younger man—" She stopped when she saw Diana blush. "I don't mean to embarrass you, so I'll say no more. I'm sure you take my meaning."

Diana shook her head. "I don't plan to remarry, Lady

Gordon. My marriage was not like yours. It was a miserable experience that I have no desire to repeat. And though Lady Regina thinks this idea of hers a good one, I can't help but distrust any man who would marry me for my fortune."

"You must realize that such a thing is a commonplace occurrence, and many times a practical one. I think Lady Regina's plan makes a lot of sense: Why not use your fortune to purchase the kind of husband you would like? You can ensure that he is nothing like your first husband was."

"I think it immoral to marry for such a reason, Lady Gordon. I will not do so again," Diana said, and Lady Gordon was taken aback by her passionate response.

"I beg your pardon—" Lady Gordon started to say, when Diana interrupted her, putting her hand out in a gesture of apology.

"No; it is *I* who must beg *your* pardon. I am far too sensitive about such matters, I know."

"Not at all; if you feel so strongly then I'm sure you have good reason to do so." Lady Gordon paused and looked searchingly at Diana before speaking again, a little hesitantly. "Forgive me, I have no wish to intrude on your private concerns, but I hope your husband did not . . . harm you in any way."

"Oh, no! Mr. Boyle was not very kind to me, but neither did he abuse me. Not physically, at any rate."

"I'm sorry he was unkind to you, but I am relieved to hear that you were not a victim of physical abuse. It's terrible how the courts allow husbands to mistreat their wives with impunity. Some of the poor women one meets when involved in charitable activities—" Lady Gordon finished her sentence with a shudder and a mournful shake of her head.

"Many have been terribly mistreated, I know. Really, I have nothing to complain of when compared to them," Diana said.

"That's not true, Diana. We all have our particular burdens to bear, and one person's suffering doesn't negate the suffering of another person. Just because there are many unfortunate and terribly mistreated people in the world does not mean that *you* are not allowed to mourn the loss of your mother or regret the unhappiness of your first marriage. There is no contest for such things and, really, if there were, who would want to be the winner? We should all be trying to alleviate one another's pain, not denying one another or ourselves the right to feel it."

Lady Regina walked into the drawing room just as Lady Gordon was finishing her speech, and she was somewhat startled by the atmosphere that prevailed there. She hesitated just inside the door, looking from Lady Gordon's serious face to Diana's moisture-filled eyes.

"I beg your pardon. Am I intruding?"

Diana laughed, and quickly dried her eyes with her handkerchief. "Regina, you're the best hostess that ever was! Here we sit, in your drawing room, and you ask if *you're* intruding. No, of course you're not. Lady Gordon was just giving me some very wise advice."

"Oh, dear. That makes me sound like an officious busybody," Lady Gordon protested, but she was smiling as well, and Regina came into the room and sat down, and the conversation soon turned to less serious matters.

MAXWELL, LIKE THE Ladies of the Registry, had also been enjoying unprecedented popularity since the ball. It had become an open secret in London society that he was the creator of the directory; however, rather than causing him to be rejected, he'd found himself flooded with invitations and treated as something of a celebrity whenever he ventured out. He was also the recipient of further visits to his rooms by mysterious young ladies. (Jim, the young porter who admitted them, was inclined to look at Maxwell in amazed curiosity, as if wondering how this unassuming gentleman had achieved such amorous success.)

The goal of these ladies, however, was the exact opposite of what Diana's had been: they did not wish to be *removed* from his directory, but rather inserted into it.

"Mr. Dean, what is the minimum amount required for inclusion in your directory?" one buxom, ruddy-cheeked young woman asked him. "If ten thousand is not enough, Pa can raise more. We own a brewery in Norfolk and our barley crop did very well this year. I'm sure plenty of young gentlemen would be happy to have unlimited access to ale. Maybe you should list *that* in the directory, next to my dowry," she said, with a hearty guffaw.

Still smiling, she moved from the chair he'd originally led her to and seated herself very near to him on the sofa. "Do *you* like ale, Mr. Dean?" she asked in a husky whisper, leaning in so close that Maxwell became concerned her impressive bosom was about to brush against his own. He immediately jumped up and retreated across the room. She'd arrived with only a footman in attendance and had ordered the servant to wait in the hall, and Max had no desire to be found with the brewer's daughter, unchaperoned, sitting chest-to-chest on a sofa. It was true he rarely had callers, but he hadn't expected this one, either. He cursed his bad timing, having been surprised by her visit just as he'd opened the door to leave and thus unable to claim he was not at home. He wished now he'd thought of some other excuse to deny her admittance, but she had hustled her way inside before he'd had a chance to think.

"I am sorry, Miss . . ." he responded, before stumbling to a halt as he realized he did not even know whom he was addressing.

"Thimblethorpe. Sylvia Thimblethorpe. Do you wish to know the spelling for your directory? It is *T-h-i—*"

"Miss Thimblethorpe, please, I do not mean to interrupt, but there will be no reprinting of the directory, so it is unnecessary for you to spell your name for me." Max thought he'd go mad before she got to the end of *that* interminable surname.

"But—" she started to protest.

"And I do beg your pardon, but I really must go," he said, crossing back to the sofa and holding his arm out to her so that she had no choice but to take it and rise to her feet. "I am late for an appointment."

Max led her, still protesting, to the door. After waving down a hackney, helping her inside, and watching it leave, he turned to address Jim. "Do not allow any other ladies into the building without my express permission," he told him.

"Must be a nice problem to have, Mister," Jim replied, looking Max up and down with a critical eye, as if trying to figure out what the attraction could be.

Max did not attempt an explanation, unconcerned with the young man's opinion of his desirability. He was much more concerned with Mrs. Boyle's opinion of him, and it was with her that he had an appointment that morning.

Not only did Mrs. Boyle not know how to ride, she had also mentioned she wanted to learn to drive, and he had quickly offered to instruct her. He told himself he was doing so to make up for his thoughtless behavior in publishing the directory, but he knew he was deceiving himself. He merely wanted an excuse to continue seeing her.

DIANA WAS BECOMING an expert at self-deception as well. She claimed she had no romantic interest in Mr. Dean and absolutely no intention of getting married again, but she took every opportunity she was offered to be in his company, though she frequently turned down invitations from other gentlemen. She, Mr. Dean, Lady Regina, and Lord Jerome had gone twice on excursions together, Lord Jerome having very clearly transferred his attentions to Regina.

But this morning Diana would be alone with Mr. Dean for the very first time since she'd made his acquaintance, as the curricle he'd hired in order to teach her to drive only held two. And he had purposely timed their outing before noon to avoid the fashionable crowd.

After picking Diana up from Lady Regina's townhouse, he drove her to the park, explaining to her the features of their hired vehicle, while comparing it point by point with a phaeton, tilbury, and stanhope. He knew she was considering purchasing a carriage and wanted her to make an informed decision. However, Diana comprehended very little of his explanation, so overwhelmed was she to be riding in a curricle with a gentleman. She had never been on a drive in an open carriage with any man, not even her late husband, who had thought the possession of a sporting carriage that only carried two persons the height of frivolity and absurdity.

Diana was not of the same opinion and thought that it

might be enjoyable for her and Lady Regina to go on drives together, especially when the weather was so pleasant and the park was bursting with color, as it was now. And though she and Mr. Dean were avoiding other people so that he could safely conduct her driving lesson, Diana found the thought of promenading on a Sunday afternoon from the seat of a curricle *she* was driving while nodding at her various acquaintances to be a thrilling prospect, indeed. She might not care about social prestige or prominence, but she and Regina did find delight in taking part in activities that they would have been excluded from only a few months previously and had agreed to enjoy their social success while it lasted.

Diana had resolved similarly regarding Mr. Dean's attentions, although her conscience sometimes bothered her, as she felt it was unfair of her to encourage him when she had no intention of marrying him. But then she would remind herself that it was her fortune that attracted him, not her person, so she was in no danger of hurting him. However, she did wonder sometimes if he could be *that* good of an actor as to simulate such delight in her company if it was merely her bank balance that pleased him.

Today, for example, when he had helped her into the curricle, he had clasped one of her hands in his while he placed his other hand gently at the small of her back. Both this and his queries about her comfort were done with such an air of protective concern that she felt . . . cherished. It was a feeling she'd never before experienced, coupled as it was with her physical reaction to Mr. Dean's presence. She began to wonder if there were advantages to marriage that she hadn't previously considered, since while she'd been married to Mr. Boyle he had rarely touched her, nor had she wanted him to.

Mr. Dean's thoughts must have been running upon similar lines, because he suddenly said, "You must have been very young when you were first married."

"I had just turned eighteen," Diana said. Her smile faded and she sat up straighter in the seat, rigid and tense, her usual reaction whenever she was asked about her marriage.

"And you were made a widow at a young age as well," Mr. Dean said sympathetically. "I am very sorry for your loss."

Diana had schooled herself to accept such condolences with a polite expression of thanks or a gracious nod of the head, but she found those niceties eluded her at that moment. "You need not be sorry. I am far happier as a widow than I ever was as a wife," she replied, so weary of hiding her true feelings that she tactlessly blurted them out.

Seeing Mr. Dean's shocked expression, Diana figured she had lost any respect he might have had for her so there was no longer any need to guard her tongue as she had trained herself to do these many months. "Now you see, Mr. Dean, why I was so opposed to your directory. My marriage, as you so rightly assumed at our first meeting, was one of financial necessity, and my only hope of escape from that union was death; either mine or my husband's. You cannot know how it feels to wish for freedom so fervently that you cannot grieve the death of another. Indeed, my primary emotion upon his death was relief."

Diana could not look at Mr. Dean; she was too ashamed, and therefore stared straight ahead, her gaze focused unseeingly on a flowering rhododendron, its bright pink flowers an indistinct blur. The silence felt unbearably tense and heavy, but Diana could not bring herself to break it, as she already regretted revealing her darkest, ugliest secrets, and felt she might lose her composure completely if she spoke again. She was surprised when Mr. Dean brought the horses to a stand and reached out to cover her hand with his own.

"I am truly sorry that your marriage was an unhappy one. And I regret more than I can ever express that I added to your pain by listing your name in the directory," he said. "But you should not continue to berate yourself for the very natural feeling of relief you experienced at the ending of a miserable situation. It's true that I have not known you very long, but I feel certain you did nothing to hasten your husband's death, and probably what you could to prevent it."

"Naturally I did all that I could! It was a very sudden attack, but then he was bedridden for weeks afterward. He had the best of physicians; I even called in a doctor from town. I tried everything . . ." Diana said, her voice breaking off as tears threatened again to overcome her.

"I have no doubt that you did. You must stop blaming yourself for something that was beyond your control." And raising her hand to his lips, he bestowed a kiss on her wrist, which peeked out from above the clasp of her short kid gloves.

The breath caught in Diana's throat, and she finally turned to look at him. The expression in his eyes was so very sympathetic that Diana felt as if the ache that seemed to be a permanent part of her, the guilt she'd carried for so long, was lessening the longer Mr. Dean looked at her. She felt a burst of gratitude and affection for him and wished she was brave enough to return his kiss. But the brazenness of that thought caused her to be overcome with shyness and broke the spell he seemed to have cast over her. She lowered her eyes from his and gently withdrew her hand.

He seemed to come to his senses as well, for he cleared his throat before saying in a hearty tone of voice: "Perhaps it's time for you to take the reins, Mrs. Boyle. It appears that this is a quiet part of the park, well suited for you to practice in safety."

Diana was relieved at the change of subject and threw herself wholeheartedly into the driving lessons. She found them quite enjoyable, but was unable to tell if the acceleration of her heartbeat was caused by the excitement of controlling a matched team of horses or the enforced proximity with Mr. Dean.

It was only later, after the lessons were finished and Mr.

Dean was in possession of the reins once again, that Diana returned to the subject they'd previously discussed.

"Thank you, Mr. Dean, for your great kindness to me this morning. You must be regretting your offer to teach me to drive. I'm sure you had little expectation, when you did so, that I would make you the recipient of uninvited, and most likely unwanted, confidences," she said, with a wry smile.

"On the contrary, I am honored," he said. "And it helps me understand better your strong feelings about your inclusion in the directory." There was a pause as Mr. Dean exchanged nods with an acquaintance who passed them on horseback before he continued: "I've wanted to explain to you for some time, Mrs. Boyle, that I did not compile that directory because I think of marriage as a glorified business transaction. That is not at all how I view marriage, and it pained me to know that I gave you that impression." He glanced over at Diana, who did not interrupt him and whose expression encouraged him to continue. "I know many younger sons, like myself, who greatly desire to marry and start a family but are prevented by their circumstances from doing so. I merely thought that if one of those gentlemen met a lady of fortune whom he did esteem highly enough for marriage, and vice versa, then there would be no obstacle to their being wed. And perhaps a younger son, like myself, who would otherwise be destined to lead a solitary, lonely life, might instead find himself the companion of the loveliest, sweetest, most charming woman he had ever met—" He broke off suddenly, and cast Diana a sheepish look.

"I am speaking generally, of course," he said, with a self-mocking smile.

"Of course," she agreed, though she treasured this description she did not think she was incorrect in assuming to be of her. And she wondered if marriage, when one was able to carefully select a mate, might not be such an awful institution after all.

9

Since neither Diana nor Mr. Dean had any desire to curtail their time together, Diana eagerly agreed to Mr. Dean's suggestion that they go by Gunter's before he returned her to Lady Regina's townhouse. This was not Diana's first visit to the tea shop and confectionery, as Lady Gordon lived just across from it in Berkeley Square, and Diana and Regina would frequently leave Lady Gordon's after a visit and walk across to Gunter's for tea or one of their famous ices. But Diana had yet to sit in a carriage with a gentleman under the plane trees while their refreshments were brought to them by an obliging waiter, as she did this day.

While they waited for their food to arrive, Mr. Dean pointed out a nearby townhome. "One of your former neighbors from Twickenham, Horace Walpole, lived there before his death," he said.

"Horace Walpole, the author?" Diana took a closer look at the stately townhouse that seemed indistinguishable from those that surrounded it. "It seems rather subdued in comparison with Strawberry Hill House."

"So, you've visited his famous Gothic mansion? What did you think of it?" Mr. Dean asked.

"It's absolutely magnificent, though a tad overwhelming. I couldn't imagine living there."

"I've heard that Walpole described the house as being imprinted with the 'gloomth' of abbeys and cathedrals, but that he wanted the gardens to laugh with the gaiety of nature."

"What a lovely thought," Diana replied. "About the gardens, I mean. I much prefer laughter to gloomth," she hurried to add, with a little laugh of her own. "That's a peculiar word. Gloomth," she repeated slowly, and then smiled at the sound of it, turning to Mr. Dean with a look of shy inquiry. "I don't think I've ever heard it before. Is it actually a word, or am I just ignorant?"

"You're not at all ignorant; I believe Mr. Walpole invented it," Mr. Dean said. He didn't know which was more tempting: Diana's smile or the way she had puckered her delectable lips while trying to pronounce that ridiculous word.

"Is Strawberry Hill House near your own?" he asked hurriedly, as he suddenly realized that he had been staring at her mouth, and the silence had begun to grow awkward. She looked relieved at his innocuous question.

"Very near. It's a pleasant walk, and I do enjoy the gardens there, though at times I arrive at Strawberry Hill and there are such crowds that I immediately return home, happy for the privacy of my own garden."

"Do you prefer solitude, then?" he asked, pleased to be gaining further insight into her character. He was also pleased that the metaphorical wall she'd erected between them seemed to be coming down. "Or are you enjoying the sociable life you've been living since you came to town?"

Diana paused and looked contemplative, as if she wondered at the answer to that question herself. "I was *accustomed* to solitude, I think," she said slowly. "I wouldn't say that I prefer it. I've been much happier since coming to town." She smiled at him in a manner that seemed to imply that *he* had something to do with her increased enjoyment, though he wondered if he was deceiving himself by believing so.

They were interrupted at that moment by the delivery of their sweets, and afterward the conversation centered primarily on the quality of the food as they happily ate their muffins and biscuits. They had just finished when they heard someone calling and looked over to see Mr. Pryce with Miss Jarmyn on his arm. Maxwell and Diana got down from the curricle and joined the other couple in a walk around the square.

Diana had learned to laugh at Mr. Pryce rather than become exasperated by him, and she was amused to find that he had fulfilled Lady Regina's prophecy: he had switched from one indecipherable form of speech to another, equally unintelligible to Diana, but which caused Miss Jarmyn to gaze at him with fawning adoration.

"'Ey up, 'ow do?" he said to Max, after Diana had exchanged greetings with Miss Jarmyn.

"Very well, indeed," Mr. Dean replied, with a smile at Diana that acknowledged Mr. Pryce's ludicrous behavior. Diana, who had never had a man read her thoughts so accurately, suddenly felt something much deeper than the amusement she'd been feeling at Mr. Pryce's antics. She experienced a surprising sense of discovery, as if she'd found something she hadn't even known she'd been looking for. She had no idea that a man and a woman could communicate a thought, even share a humorous moment, merely with a meeting of their eyes. But she shook those thoughts away for another time, as she realized the conversation had come to a halt while she was staring at Mr. Dean in amazement, and that she hadn't contributed to it at all other than a "How do you do?" to Miss Jarmyn. She turned away from Mr. Dean and asked Mr. Pryce: "Did you and Miss Jarmyn have refreshments at Gunter's as well?"

"We did reet enough, choose how," Mr. Pryce said, with a glance at Miss Jarmyn, who nodded in confirmation; whether at his statement or his correct use of Yorkshire dialect, Diana did not know. But she was glad to see that Miss Jarmyn and Mr. Pryce understood each other so well. She was beginning to recognize how rare and pre-cious a thing that was.

AFTER RETURNING TO Regina's, Diana was surprised to be met at the door and told by the butler that Lady Regina was entertaining callers in the drawing room, and that she had requested Diana join them immediately upon her re-turn. But when Diana neared the room, her surprise turned to dismay when she heard Mildred's piercing tones, inter-spersed by the lower tones of a masculine voice she did not recognize.

Taking a deep, steadying breath outside the door and telling herself Mildred had no power over her, Diana squared her shoulders and entered the drawing room.

The inhabitants of the room rose at her entrance, and Mildred was indeed there with Lady Regina, accompanied by a gentleman whom Diana did not know. He smiled at her very pleasantly and cordially, his expression in stark contrast to the frown that graced Mildred's face, and Di-ana told herself that was undoubtedly the reason she felt he looked *too* happy to see her.

He was dressed in a gentlemanly fashion, although not as stylishly as the men Diana had been associating with since coming to town. It was obvious this man was not a city buck, and also, from the worn gloves she'd seen resting on the entry table, that he was of less fortunate

circumstances than even the younger sons who frequented the balls and parlors of the Ladies of the Registry.

His appearance was not unpleasant, most women
might even call him handsome, but something about the
man caused Diana to feel an instinctive distrust. Perhaps
it was merely because he accompanied Mildred, which
seemed a suspicious thing in itself. Diana had lived with
Mildred for nearly seven years, and any acquaintance of
hers Diana had perforce become acquainted with as well.
Yet Diana had never seen this man before in her life.

"Diana, there you are. We have been waiting for you
for quite some time," Mildred said, annoyed.

"I am sorry for that, Mildred, but since I did not know
you were coming, I cannot be blamed for the length of
time you have been waiting," Diana said, in as pleasant a
tone as she could muster. "Won't you introduce me to
your companion?"

Diana had no idea why these words seemed to afford
Mildred so much amusement. "Mrs. Boyle," Mildred said
with a titter, "allow me to introduce you to *Mr. Boyle*." She
paused, seemingly savoring the moment of surprise before adding: "Mr. Lucius Boyle; Mrs. Diana Boyle."

Mr. Boyle bowed and Diana nodded her head in
response. She was proud of herself for her unflustered reaction; she even managed a slight smile. Still, she was
enormously relieved when Lady Regina took charge, inviting everyone to sit before turning to offer Diana an explanation. "It appears that Mr. Boyle is the nephew of Miss

Boyle and your late husband, and went to America fifteen years ago at the age of sixteen."

"He was Percival's favorite relation," Mildred stated in a challenging tone of voice, as if she expected Diana to contradict her.

"I was disconsolate to hear of my uncle's death," Mr. Boyle said, assuming a suitably mournful expression, which seemed as false to Diana as his prior expression of delight. "I am very sorry for your loss," he told Diana in a quiet aside, leaning toward her and bestowing upon her a look of sympathy that was, in Diana's opinion, overly intimate for someone she had only just met.

Mildred made a noise deep in her throat that she transformed into a cough, and Diana was grateful Mildred had contented herself with that expression of her distaste and had swallowed whatever insulting remark she had intended to make about Diana being unworthy of sympathy, having been a very poor excuse for a wife and an even worse widow.

"So, you last saw Mr. Boyle fifteen years ago, Mildred? You must be very pleased to meet him again, after all these years," Diana said, eager to change the subject.

"Call me Cousin Lucius, please. And perhaps I could call you Cousin Diana?" Lucius asked. "It seems odd to refer to you as Mrs. Boyle, which is the name I associate with my mother. And I'm sure you dislike repeatedly hearing the name you associate with your dear departed husband as well."

While this was undoubtedly true, Diana had no desire to be addressed by her Christian name by this man, whether or not the word "cousin" preceded it. "How long a visit to England do you intend to make?" she asked, hoping what they called each other would prove to be a moot topic as this would be their one—and only—meeting.

"Lucius intends on settling in England again. He's all alone in the world; we are the only family he has. I've invited him to stay at Whitley House," Mildred said, with a barely concealed look of triumph. "I knew, fond as you were of my brother, you'd never deny one of his dearest relations a place to stay."

"Your generosity overwhelms me, Aunt," Lucius said to Mildred, with a bow in her direction. "Of course, if Cousin Diana does not wish for me to stay . . ."

Politeness prevented Diana from agreeing with him, and she spoke before the silence could grow too awkward. "I am sure I can have no objection to you staying at Whitley House while I am in town," she said, hoping to convey by her statement that she expected him to leave upon her return.

"But Diana, that is why we came to call. To tell you that you must curtail your stay and return to Whitley House at once," Mildred said. "Percival would have wanted you to show hospitality to his favorite relation. If Lucius had returned to England before Percival's death, or if Percival had known his direction—well, who knows how matters might have turned out. Lucius might now be master at Whitley House, and we *his* guests."

Lucius responded with a humble shake of his head and a murmured, "Now, Aunt, that is kind of you to say, but I had no such expectations. And I am pleased to be the guest of my lovely cousin." He smiled and bowed to Diana.

"At any rate," Mildred continued, ignoring Lucius's interruption, "it would be quite outrageous to have your cousin stay and not be there yourself to ensure his needs were met."

Diana was once again thankful for Regina's intervention because, while Diana's mouth had opened, she felt as if she couldn't produce any words. Or at least any that could be spoken in polite society. She'd never felt more tempted to borrow from her deceased father's vocabulary.

"But Miss Boyle, it would be just as outrageous for Diana to leave *me* before her visit has ended," Regina said, in a sugary tone that just barely hid the steel underneath. "She's promised to stay for another month at least, and I don't intend to allow her to break that promise."

"Nonsense. That was before she knew her cousin had come. Obviously the situation has changed and she can be released from any so-called promise." A roll of the eyes punctuated this remark, making it clear that Mildred was all but calling her hostess a liar.

"I would be happy to wait upon my cousin here, and escort her back to her home whenever she is ready to return," Mr. Boyle remarked, with another of his incessant bows.

"That is very accommodating of you, Mr. Boyle, but I could not deprive Mildred of your company," Diana said. She then jumped up from her seat, which meant Mr. Boyle had no choice but to stand as well, protesting as he did so that he thought they'd agreed to dispense with titles. Diana ignored this remark and continued: "Thank you so very much for calling, but we cannot keep you any longer. Lady Regina and I have a prior appointment."

"So we do," Regina said, moving over to Miss Boyle's side and putting a hand under her arm to encourage her to rise from her chair, as she still had made no move to do so. "Mr. Boyle, Miss Boyle, so delighted to have made your acquaintance."

"But—nothing has been decided . . . Diana, you are coming home, are you not? We need not inconvenience Lady Regina; I can send our coachman with the carriage tomorrow," Mildred said to Diana over her shoulder, as Regina ushered her to the door.

"I will write to you when I am ready, so do not bother sending the carriage until you receive word," Diana said. Mildred continued to protest the entire way out of the room, with Mr. Boyle punctuating her remarks with unctuous requests to be of assistance to his "Cousin Diana."

When the door finally closed behind their troublesome guests, Diana and Regina fell with a sigh upon the sofa.

Diana took out some of her frustration by pummeling a defenseless pillow, but when a feather escaped a busted seam and floated sadly to the floor, she turned to look at Regina in apology. "I'm so sorry. I'll buy you another."

"My mother made that for me," Regina said.

Diana was appalled. "Oh, no! It can be mended—"

Regina laughed. "I was teasing you, Diana. I'm actually more than a little relieved that you hit the pillow and not your sister-in-law."

"I'll never be quit of that woman." Diana slumped back onto the sofa, forgetting all the deportment lessons of her childhood, and was relieved Mildred wasn't there to tell her to sit up straight. "She is the one thing that could make me consider marrying again," Diana said, and was not entirely sure she was joking.

"That might be a case of jumping out of the frying pan into the fire. It appears to me that Miss Boyle *wants* you to marry again, but to a man of her choosing. I suspect she's trying her hand at a little matchmaking."

"You mean Cousin Lucius, I suppose," Diana said.

"The very same. And he doesn't appear averse to the idea either," Regina said.

"Why would he be? He would gain possession of Whitley House and a tidy fortune to go along with it."

"And he's probably assured his dear 'Aunt Mildred' she can remain there permanently if she helps him succeed in his aim," Regina said. "If you were to marry again, as

Mildred obviously fears you might, someone else may not be as inclined to have her as a permanent guest. Perhaps this is her way of securing her future."

"I cannot pretend to be any better than either of them. I married a cousin for money and a home; why shouldn't Lucius Boyle attempt to do the same? It seems that emigrating to America did not improve his fortunes. He looks to be as impoverished as I used to be."

"Don't start feeling sorry for him," Regina warned Diana. "For all you know he lost his money at the gaming tables. It's not your responsibility to marry him just because you were once forced into a marriage of convenience yourself. You were a young girl of eighteen and he is a hale and hearty man of thirty, at least. Your circumstances are entirely different."

"I do wonder, though, if Mildred is right, and if my hus— Mr. Boyle had known Lucius was alive, he would have left Whitley House to him. I have no doubt he'd have much preferred to have left it to a male relation," Diana said.

"If they were so close, why did Lucius not write to Mr. Boyle and provide him with his direction? It's a convenient fiction that Mildred's invented to work on your conscience, which she knows to be tender in this regard."

The women subsided into contemplation, their "appointment" forgotten, until Diana broke the silence with a quiet laugh. Regina looked at her in surprise, one brow raised. "I was just thinking," Diana explained with a smile, "the other thing that tempts me to marry again is the thought of changing my surname. I was born a Boyle, and then married one, and it is not the most melodious of names. And yet, if your theory is correct, Cousin Lucius wishes to offer me the opportunity to become a Boyle for a third time."

Regina chuckled. "That settles it, then. We must look for a prospective husband for you with an attractive surname in addition to an attractive appearance. What say you to a shorter name, of fewer syllables?" Regina asked with a grin.

Diana smiled back, having no need to inquire to which name Regina referred. Although Diana was aware that Mr. Dean had proven himself as determined a fortune hunter as Lucius Boyle likely was, she gave in to temptation and repeated "Diana Dean" and "Mrs. Dean" silently to herself and had to acknowledge it was a decided improvement over "Mrs. Boyle."

THE LADIES OF the Registry met the next morning at Lady Gordon's house and, once they'd all settled into chairs and sofas and the chatter had died down, Lady Regina addressed them. "It seems a long time since our first meeting, though it was little more than a month ago that we decided to band together and turn the tables on the gentlemen who sought to marry us for our fortunes," she said. "How do you all feel matters are progressing?"

There was a brief silence that Mrs. Young broke, her voice tentative. "I am sorry, Lady Regina, but I found myself unable to do all that you suggested."

"In what respect?" Regina asked.

"I have no desire to trifle with some poor man's affections, or lead him on with no thought of marriage. It is not in my nature."

"Mrs. Young, there is no need to apologize! You are not obligated to do anything at all; it was only a suggestion for those who find they do not wish to marry. I merely thought that we should have the same freedom the gentlemen have, to withdraw from a relationship without having to pay a penalty for it. I did not want any lady to feel compelled to wed against her will."

Mrs. Young nodded her understanding with a relieved smile, and Miss Ballard, who was a bit of a flirt, piped up. "I have no problem trifling with any number of gentlemen's affections. If they want my fortune, let them earn it. And if any of you ladies have suitors to spare, you're welcome to send them my way." She smiled saucily at the rest of the ladies and there was some laughter but also some protests that Miss Ballard had more than enough attention as it was.

After the room had quieted, Regina looked around and asked: "How about the rest of you? How do you feel about what has transpired since our first meeting?"

"I do think that my confidence has improved," Miss Meadows said. "I'm not as anxious about gaining a gentleman's approval, but rather, I now expect him to make an effort to win mine." Miss Meadows had at one time been known by the cruel sobriquet "Mousy Meadows," and her fortune had been considered her most attractive attribute. However, the past weeks she had indeed grown in confidence, which had the effect of making her other attributes more obvious. She was intelligent and kind, and had a beautiful voice, which was heard far more often now that she had the confidence to speak up and people were actually listening to her.

"It's been liberating not to have to worry so much about what others think of me," Miss Cavendish agreed, and when Diana compared the manner and expressions of the ladies around her to how they appeared when she first met them, she realized that they seemed far less nervous and much more comfortable in their own skin. As she was herself.

"I think we've accomplished quite a lot. We've made good friends," Diana said, with a warm smile at the ladies who surrounded her, "and we've entered society upon our own terms. We've made it clear that our opinions, likes, and concerns should be valued as much as any man's. And I've even learned to drive a curricle," she added, sounding so surprised at her accomplishment that the other ladies smiled in response.

"I'm learning to fence," Miss Ballard said, and a few other ladies also mentioned a sport or activity they were studying that was typically considered to be open only to gentlemen, and Diana felt a warm rush of pride at what she and her fellow women were accomplishing.

"Thank you, Lady Regina, for turning what could have been a negative experience, our inclusion in that directory, into a positive one," Mrs. Young said. "And I am also grateful to you, Lady Gordon, for involving us in your charitable activities. I'm happy to use the resources I possess in helping other women who are not as fortunate as we are."

There were murmurs of agreement and the conversation soon turned to charity work. Later, as the party broke up and the ladies began taking their leave, Diana overheard Miss Cavendish telling Lady Gordon she was taking dancing lessons from Monsieur de la Tour. "He asked how you were doing, Lady Gordon," Miss Cavendish said. "I think he admires you. You appeared so well matched when you danced together at the ball. I don't suppose *you* are interested in taking lessons from him?"

"At my age?" Lady Gordon scoffed. "Don't be ridiculous. I'm long past the age for dancing lessons. Or for flirtations with handsome French dancing masters," she added dryly.

"Perhaps you could ask him to be your escort to Vauxhall Gardens," Diana suggested.

"I hadn't planned on attending," Lady Gordon said, and there was an immediate outcry against that decision from the small group of ladies who were still present. "It is kind of you to ask me, and I am happy to provide support to you ladies in any way I can, but I don't think you need me to attend Vauxhall with you."

"Of course we don't *need* you to, Lady Gordon, we *want* you to," Diana said.

Lady Gordon smiled reminiscently. "I haven't been to Vauxhall in years. Lord Gordon took me the very first time I went. That's actually where—" Her voice broke and she couldn't finish her sentence, and Diana and Regina exchanged sympathetic glances. It was obvious some significant event in Lord and Lady Gordon's romance had occurred at Vauxhall; perhaps it was where he had proposed or they had embraced for the first time.

"Then it is past time for you to return," Regina said, but in a tone of voice that robbed her words of any harshness.

"I don't know if I can," Lady Gordon whispered, and when she looked at them, her eyes were filled with pain. Diana recognized all too well that particular species of pain; the pain of loss.

"You *can* do it," Diana told her. "And you can create new memories there, with us."

Lady Gordon blinked away a tear, and Diana was awestruck by the beauty of her blue-green eyes; they appeared more jewellike than ever with the light reflecting off her unshed tears. And then she nodded and smiled at them, and Diana found that brave smile even more awe-inspiring. This was a *true* lady of quality; a woman of strength, courage, and integrity. Diana was proud to call her a friend.

10

THE DAY OF the Vauxhall excursion finally arrived, and Diana couldn't remember feeling this much excitement since she was a child anticipating her father's return from sea. She was even more excited about this excursion than she had been about the ball, as she'd been far too nervous that evening to truly enjoy herself, although there had been moments of joy interspersed with periods of terror. This would be Diana's first time visiting the famous pleasure gardens and, surprisingly enough, Lady Regina had never been there before, either. While Vauxhall had been popular with Londoners from all facets of society since the first half of the previous century, it was not considered the most proper of entertainments for unmarried young ladies. But since most of their group were past their teen years, and some were widows of unsullied reputation, this seemed a perfect opportunity to go; especially when they had gentlemen accompanying them to protect them from any nefarious characters who might be present.

In preparation for their visit, Diana and Regina had diligently studied the novels of Frances Burney, in which poor Evelina was attacked by libertines on one of the dark walks, and a drunken acquaintance of Cecilia's shot himself near the supper boxes. They both felt that, having done such meticulous research, they could avoid the absolute worst dangers that might exist in the gardens: the dramatic scenarios invented by a lady author.

Their group was too large to travel together; fourteen of the ladies were coming, accompanied by fifteen gentlemen. (There was one extra gentleman because Miss Ballard had insisted upon *two* escorts.) They had therefore planned to travel to Vauxhall in smaller groups and meet at the Orchestra at eight o'clock. Diana's group was composed of her five favorite people: Lady Gordon and Regina, with their escorts Monsieur de la Tour and Lord Jerome, and Diana's escort, Mr. Dean.

While it was possible to travel there by coach (and with the completion of the Vauxhall Bridge last year, that was the most convenient method), they decided to take a boat across the Thames. Even though Diana lived on the river, she found the prospect of crossing it by wherry on an excursion to the pleasure gardens in the company of three handsome gentlemen very thrilling, as did Lady Regina. And Lady Gordon was pleased to observe the excitement of the younger ladies. (Though she'd arranged for her coach-man to be waiting for them at the Coach Gate on Kennington Lane later that evening when it was time to leave.)

When Diana asked Monsieur de la Tour to accompany them to provide an escort for Lady Gordon, she explained to him that Lady Gordon had last visited Vauxhall with her late husband and that she may be saddened by her memories of him.

"Poor lady," Monsieur de la Tour said sympathetically. "It is no easy matter to go on living when those you love are gone." And Diana realized that he must have experienced much loss in his own life, surviving a revolution in France and escaping to England alone. "I will take the ut-most care of her," he promised, and Diana, observing him that evening, felt he was very diligent in fulfilling his responsibility. He was very jealous of his role, not allowing any of the other gentlemen to hand Lady Gordon in and out of the carriage or the boat and treating her as if she were made of porcelain.

Lady Gordon accepted such treatment with the grace and dignity with which she always conducted herself, and Diana was pleased to see that she appeared to be in a cheerful mood, not seeming too troubled, at least not outwardly, by sad memories.

It was a tad chilly on the river, even though it was the end of June and the days had grown warmer and longer. Diana shivered as she was struck by a particularly strong breeze, and Mr. Dean drew closer to her, trying to shield her from the wind with his body. Diana felt warmth infuse her almost immediately, but she was unsure if it was because Mr. Dean had successfully blocked the cool breeze, or because she was so affected by his consideration (and proximity).

Finally they arrived, and after they paid the entrance fee and entered through the Water Gate, Diana and Regina looked around them in wonder, feeling Vauxhall Gardens not only met but exceeded their expectations. While Frances Burney's Evelina allowed that the gardens were "very pretty," she complained that they were too formal, and that she would have been "better pleased if it consisted less of straight walks." Diana felt the opposite. The neat rows of trees covered in multicolored lanterns, the arches and porticos and piazzas, the beautiful sculptures, some life-sized, scattered throughout the gardens; all of this made Diana feel as if she'd been transferred to a foreign land. There was obvious inspiration from Italy, with the Italian walks, Palladian architecture, colonnades, and loggias; and the French influence was also apparent in the elaborate interior of the Rotunda and the artwork by French artists and sculptors, such as the famous statue of Handel by Louis-François Roubiliac. But there was also a Chinese pavilion, and a Turkish saloon, and the orchestra building, described as "Gothick," was like nothing Diana had ever seen. It was a semicircular building with three levels, the second of which held the fifty-person orchestra, and it was topped by a huge crown, brilliantly lit, modeled from the crest of the Prince of Wales. And many of the paintings, by Hayman and Hogarth, were quintessentially English: composed of rural May Days and milkmaids, scenes from Shakespeare, and British military victories. Diana had definitely entered a different land, but it was a fantasyland, not one that existed anywhere else in the world.

They had arrived nearly an hour before they were supposed to meet the others, though while walking through the gardens, they did occasionally pass some of the Ladies of the Registry and their escorts, intent on a similar exploration of the park. When this happened, they all exclaimed spontaneously and rapturously at the coincidence and were genuinely delighted to see one another. And while it was not so very unlikely a meeting (as they had obviously arranged to meet there that evening and knew they were to see one another again a mere half hour later), there were so many hundreds of people milling about that were unknown to them that it was quite thrilling to recognize a familiar face among the throngs.

While Diana's small group of six stayed within sight of one another while wandering through the gardens, a very natural separation occurred, so that the three couples were spread a small distance apart. Lady Regina and Lord Jerome, the most energetic and high-spirited of the bunch, had taken the lead, and Diana could hear them up ahead, laughing and chattering gaily. The gentlemen had visited Vauxhall before, Lord Jerome in particular having done so many times, so they were very familiar with the gardens and were pointing out their favorite aspects to the particular lady at their side. Although Diana overheard Monsieur de la Tour and Lady Gordon having a more serious conversation. It appeared Lord Gordon had been a founding member of the Wilmot Committee, which had been formed to alleviate the suffering of French émigrés to England, and had been of assistance to Monsieur de la Tour when he had arrived in London. This was before Lord and Lady Gordon had married, so she had not even been aware of her husband's involvement in the charity, but Monsieur de la Tour's mention of it led her to reminisce about him, and Monsieur listened patiently and attentively as she did so.

When Diana and Mr. Dean were out of earshot of the older couple, whose conversation had become so intense that their pace had slowed considerably, Diana brought up a matter that she'd been curious about. "Lady Gordon was quite surprised by her inclusion in your directory," she told him.

"When you say surprised, I assume you mean she was grossly offended, like you were?" he asked, smiling ruefully.

"No, that's not what I meant. I don't think she was offended; she just felt she is past the marriageable age, and so couldn't understand why you would put her on a list of prospective brides. Were you unaware of her age?"

"I don't know her exact age, and I hope I'm too gentlemanly to inquire," he said with a smile. "But I did know she was more than a decade my senior. I can understand if, like yourself, she has no desire to remarry and therefore was upset that I included her without first asking permission, but I do not feel her *age* should disqualify her from marrying again. While I had not made the acquaintance of many of the ladies in the directory, I did know Lady Gordon. I met her soon after I came to town, about seven years ago. She and Lord Gordon were my idea of what a truly successful marriage should be."

"In what way?" Diana asked, curious as to what he might consider a successful marriage.

"They appeared to have, as Shakespeare wrote, 'the marriage of true minds.' Theirs was not the typical society marriage of a Lady Oxford or Lord Yarmouth, with their dozens of lovers and 'miscellany' of children, sired by unknown fathers and born to women other than their wives. Lord and Lady Gordon seemed loyal to each other and very much in love. I greatly admired Lady Gordon, and still do. I think any man who won her hand would gain a great prize, even if she had no fortune," he said.

"But she was unable to have children," Diana said.

"That is a pity, if she desired them. But many men would prefer to find a true love like she and her husband possessed, to find that other half of their soul, whether that union resulted in children or not."

"Is that what you're looking for? The other half of your soul?" Diana asked, her heart beating tumultuously at her boldness in discussing such intimate subjects with him. She had never had a conversation like this with any man.

"I do not know what I look for," he said, and was quiet for a moment before adding: "I only know what I lack."

Diana had been too shy to look at him throughout their conversation; she had kept her gaze fixed ahead of her on the path, but now she found herself compelled to look up. As she did so, he looked down at her, and their eyes met. And she found herself feeling that she, too, had been greatly deprived.

"I wonder if it's even possible," she said, and was only half-aware she was speaking aloud.

"What?" he whispered.

"To fill that empty part of your soul."

"I cannot say for certain, but I'm beginning to suspect that it is," he told her, and pressed the hand that rested confidingly on his arm.

Lady Regina, who had flirted and joked with Lord Jerome down the entire length of the Grand Walk, suddenly realized that they had outdistanced their companions by quite an extent. Still, they had numerous chaperones in the great crowd of humanity that surrounded them; mostly consisting of those of the solid middle class, but also including a few members of the *haut ton*, who had seen

Lord Jerome and Lady Regina walking together and looked slightly astonished by the sight.

Regina, like Diana, was thoroughly enjoying the gardens, and had listened happily to Jerome's explanation of the history of some of the art and the engineering behind the waterworks. He had stopped talking and they were walking in silence, but Regina was thinking about how well-informed and intelligent he was, and how devastatingly attractive those qualities were in a man who actually knew what he was talking about. So she was taken by surprise when her companion suddenly drew her into a slight alcove off the main walk, out of sight of the crowds.

"I beg your pardon, Regina, but it just occurred to me that we might not have another opportunity like this to talk in private, and I wanted to ask you something."

Regina, startled by this announcement, tried not to let her imagination run away with her and assume he was about to make a declaration or anything resembling one. Perhaps he was interested in one of the other ladies in the directory and wanted her opinion of his chances with her. Since that thought was too terrible to contemplate, she quickly decided that it was more likely that he wanted to know what his friend Mr. Dean's chances were with Diana. Realizing that she was delaying the inevitable and that he was starting to frown at her lack of response, she finally nodded, smiled, and said: "Of course, Jerome. You can ask me anything."

He smiled back, but then immediately grew serious. "It

might be hard for you to talk about," he warned her, and her heart dropped. "I just wanted to say, I had to apologize— dash it, he didn't hurt you, did he? Because I can still challenge him, though it might be difficult for me to find him after all these years. And you'd have to tell me his name, because I can't remember it for the life of me. Was it Cassidy? Cathaway? Cavity?"

Regina was totally confused. Jerome was making absolutely no sense. And here she'd just been telling herself how intelligent he was. "I am sorry, Jerome, but I have no idea what you're talking about."

"That cad you eloped with. It occurred to me that he might have hurt you."

"I see," Regina said, and her heart melted a little at his concern. Jerome was obviously very upset, even though it had happened eleven years ago. She saw his hands trembling before he clenched them into fists, and he looked as if he couldn't decide whether to weep or murder someone. "It is very kind of you to be concerned, but my father arrived before he could—before anything happened," Regina said. She wasn't about to tell Jerome her suitor hadn't been very eager to do anything anyway. She was thrilled that he cared so much. "He didn't hurt me, but I appreciate your concern." She reached up and cupped his cheek with her hand, wanting to comfort him in some way and express the affection that had welled up inside her. She wished she had the courage to kiss him.

She was about to remove her hand, thinking that perhaps

she was embarrassing herself and he had no desire for her to touch him (and also realizing that it was a very forward thing to do), when he put his hand over hers, holding it against his face. Then, turning his head, he pressed a kiss into her palm, before lowering her hand to her side and slowly releasing it.

She was smiling at him so hard she thought her face might crack, and he was looking at her wonderingly, before he raised his hand to *her* cheek. "You have a dimple," he said, touching it briefly with his finger. "Have you always had one and I've never noticed? It's adorable."

"Only one, however," Regina said, breathlessly. "I don't have a matched set."

"It's unique; like you are," he said, not sounding nearly as quick-witted as he usually did, though Regina had no fault to find with his conversation. They stood there smiling at each other, and Regina started to wonder if he might be about to kiss her when she heard Diana calling her name.

Regina felt a little foolish stepping out of the wooded alcove where she'd obviously been secreted with Lord Jerome, but he'd regained his smooth tongue, and told the rest of the party he'd been showing Regina a rare plant, a *Sonophorus japonica.*

"I'd love to see it as well," Mr. Dean said. "Does it have bell-shaped flowers?"

"It's not in bloom at the moment," Lord Jerome said, with a glare at his friend, who apparently knew his Latin.

"Perhaps we can see it some other time," Diana said sweetly, as if she wasn't aware that Jerome had just invented it. "It's time to meet the others in our group."

As she was speaking, Lady Gordon and Monsieur de la Tour caught up with them, and they all turned to walk back to the main piazza and the orchestra building. Though if some of them wished they had not invited quite so many to the gardens that evening, they kept such thoughts to themselves.

"Mr. Pitt," Regina whispered to Lord Jerome, as they were walking.

"I beg your pardon?" he asked.

"My former beau. His name wasn't Cavity, it was Pitt," she said.

And Lord Jerome, who was known to rarely even smile, was observed that evening laughing out loud.

THEY MET THE rest of the group near the orchestra building, which was very crowded and noisy, as the band was playing. After exchanging greetings and a few introductions (as while the ladies were familiar with one another, their escorts weren't known to everyone), they all went to their assigned supper boxes.

The supper boxes were inside colonnades that lined the main walks and the central square, and Lord Jerome led their group to a box on the Grand South Walk, in a quieter part of the gardens. There were walls between the boxes, which afforded them privacy from those on either side, but each was open at the front and back, and shortly after they had sat at the dining table, a signal was given and a large painting was "let fall" at the back of the box.

Diana and Regina exclaimed at the sight of a huge painting, at least eight feet wide and five feet tall, that now formed one of the "walls" of their supper box. It displayed a trio of milkmaids dancing for their customers in a village square on May Day, their tightly corseted dresses of the previous century appearing much too rich to be worn by country milkmaids, but beautiful nonetheless. The central figure wore a dress with an intricate vine-and-floral pattern, her petticoat (and a great deal of bosom) peeking out above the cinched bodice. Her dance partner, another milkmaid, was caught mid-twirl, and wore a gown of iridescent pale pink. There were men in the painting as well: a porter carrying the "garland" and a fiddler who supplied the music for the dancing, but they did little to distract attention from the women.

After studying it carefully, Regina turned to Jerome with a teasing smile. "Did you pick this particular box so that you could gaze upon beautiful young women while you ate your slivers of ham and drank your punch?"

"Not at all. While I do like the artwork, I selected this box for its location. If I wanted to gaze upon beautiful women, I have no need to look at a painting," he said, bowing to Regina, before turning to nod at Diana and Lady Gordon.

"You notice he omitted the word 'young,'" Regina said
to the other ladies, sotto voce, but she was obviously joking.

"The setting is English, but the style seems very French,"
Monsieur de la Tour said, in reference to the painting.

"Yes, you are right," Jerome told him. "Francis Hayman,
the artist, was very influenced by the French rocaille style.
Hayman did many of the paintings in the supper boxes.
There is even one titled *See-Saw,* and I believe Fragonard
has a painting on the same subject."

"*La bascule,*" Lady Gordon translated for Monsieur de
la Tour's benefit, and he smiled at her.

"Could we see a few of the other paintings?" Diana
asked, as she was very interested in art, though her canvas
of choice was fabric and she painted with a needle. "Since
we know the inhabitants of the nearby supper boxes, it
makes a perfect excuse to take a tour."

The others liked this idea as well, and the group visited
the adjoining boxes, chatting with the other ladies and
their escorts, and viewing the paintings. They saw scenes
of pastoral England, with children and adults playing at
bird-catching and cricket, but they also found the painting
Lord Jerome had mentioned, *See-Saw,* which was in the
box where Mr. Pryce, Miss Jarmyn, Miss Ballard, and her
two noble escorts sat.

This painting was not as lighthearted as many of the
others; the colors were darker, and while the young men
and women were at play, it appeared as if something omi-
nous was about to occur. The seesaw looked to be rather

haphazardly constructed, and was near a building sur-rounded by scaffolding.

"Looks more like a battle scene than fun and games," Mr. Pryce said, surprising everyone (except Miss Jarmyn) with this sensible observation.

"Some of Hayman's paintings were very moralistic, at the urging of the first manager of the gardens," Jerome explained.

"And what is the moral of this one?" Miss Ballard asked. "Don't play on seesaws?"

"Perhaps it's a warning to young ladies not to play with more than one gentleman," Miss Jarmyn said, frank as usual. Diana and Regina exchanged a glance at Miss Jarmyn's outspokenness. They realized Miss Ballard couldn't help but feel those words applied to her, the only lady in their group with two gentlemen escorts.

"Then I'd better study it diligently, hadn't I?" Miss Ballard said, apparently unperturbed by Miss Jarmyn's remark, and she rose from her seat to walk closer to the painting.

Diana moved closer to the painting, too, and found that she agreed with Miss Jarmyn's explanation. A young man and woman sat on opposite sides of the seesaw, the boy suspended high in the air, the girl down low. How-ever, the innocent scene was made somewhat shocking by the fact that the young woman was half lying in the arms of a different young man who had caught her on her de-scent, and who was now holding the seesaw down with one foot so it did not move as he embraced her. Another young man, a bystander, had his fists clenched and looked to be running toward the girl and her embracer. And the others in the painting watched with horror-stricken expressions, either because they thought a fight was about to break out or the seesaw would collapse with the other boy's extra weight.

"It does appear that the young lady is *toying* with two men's affections," Mr. Dean said, but since his awful pun lightened the atmosphere and directed attention away from Miss Ballard, Diana was very grateful for it, and laughed harder than the joke deserved.

The waiter arrived just then with the other party's food, and Diana's group used it as an opportunity to return to their own box and escape the slightly awkward atmosphere of the other. Their meal soon arrived as well, and as it had now grown dark, there was soon a whistle and the lamplighters lit the thousands of lanterns.

This felt miraculous to Diana, as they all seemed to light up at once, and Mr. Dean explained to her that it was because cotton wool fuses had been set up during the day so that when a lantern was lit, the flame automatically traveled from one oil lamp to another.

Diana thought Vauxhall Gardens was a veritable feast for the senses, between the beautiful trees and walks, the artwork, and the music from orchestras playing in several venues throughout the park and which could still be heard, though not too loudly, in their supper box. Diana even found nothing to complain about as regards the food, though she'd heard others joke about how thinly the ham was shaved and how watered down the punch was. Diana thought it was just as well the punch wasn't very potent, because she was already so overwhelmed by her surroundings and their beauty that she felt intoxicated by them, and did not think she could handle any further stimulation of her senses.

But just as she had decided this was the most memorable and enjoyable evening of her life, as well as the most romantic, something occurred to greatly lessen her enjoyment.

A number of people had passed in front of their supper box as the group ate and occasionally one or two would call out to Lord Jerome, Lady Gordon, or Mr. Dean, who would exchange nods, and sometimes greetings, with these acquaintances. Lady Regina and Diana knew fewer people in London, and most of those they'd met through Lady Gordon, so she was usually greeted first. Therefore, Diana was very surprised, and annoyed, to hear her name being called by a lone gentleman. She was finally enjoying a private tête-à-tête with Mr. Dean (the other two couples having left to resume their exploration of the gardens) and was not happy to have been interrupted. "Cousin Diana! What an unexpected surprise to see you again so soon," the man said loudly.

It was Lucius Boyle, smiling in a way Diana persisted in feeling was disingenuous, though what reason he would have to pretend to be pleased to see her she couldn't imagine. She felt, however, that their meeting was not "unexpected," nor was he "surprised" to see her.

Diana nodded at him but didn't speak, hoping that her lack of enthusiasm at seeing him would discourage him and he would leave. But she should have realized that it would not be that easy. He came into their box, saying apologetically, "I beg your pardon for interrupting your supper. Allow me to order another bowl of punch."

"No, Mr. Boyle, that will not be necessary; we have just finished eating and were about to walk through the gardens," Diana said, still hoping he would take the hint his company was unwelcome.

"Cousin Diana, how many times must I ask you to call me Cousin Lucius?" he gently chided her. "And I don't believe I'm acquainted with your companion," he said, turning his glance expectantly toward Maxwell Dean.

Maxwell could tell by Diana's expression that this man's presence was unwanted, but she did not deny that he was her cousin, and Max did not feel that he should be rude to a member of Mrs. Boyle's family. So he acknowledged the introduction in a polite, though distant, manner, and was relieved to hear the bell that signaled the ten o'clock showing of the Cascade.

"I do beg your pardon, Mr. Boyle," he said, "but I had promised to take Mrs. Boyle to see the waterworks."

Diana hopped up eagerly, as she had been greatly looking forward to this treat, but Mr. Boyle somehow took this as an invitation to accompany them. Though Diana held firmly on to Mr. Dean's arm (especially as the crowds grew in number) and tried her best to ignore Mr. Boyle, he stuck like a barnacle to her other side.

They finally met up with the other members of their party at the Cascade and Diana and Mr. Dean were able to separate themselves from Mr. Boyle at last, though Diana could still see him on the periphery of the group, struggling to make his way back to her side. The press of people had forced her and Mr. Dean even closer to each other; he was standing behind her and her back now rested against his chest. He touched her nowhere else, but Diana felt as if he were forming a protective shield, keeping her safe from Mr. Boyle and anyone else who would bother her. Once again she felt intoxicated, giddy with nervous excitement and pleasure, especially as Mr. Dean began to speak into her ear. He was merely explaining to her the features of the Cascade, but he could have been reciting Samuel Johnson's dictionary to her and it would have been just as exciting, as the breathy whisper in her ear was causing the most delightful tickling sensation. Still, she struggled to pay attention to what he was saying and to the sight in front of her, as it was like nothing she'd ever seen before.

The Vauxhall workers had raised a curtain, and behind it was a painted landscape of a bridge with a water mill. This mill was magically turned by a cascade, or waterfall. But there was no water, as much as it looked and sounded as if there were. Mr. Dean explained it was manufactured from pieces of tin affixed to two wheels and illuminated by hidden lights. At the same time you "saw" the water-fall, you heard the sound of running water. There were even coaches, wagons, and people to be seen crossing the bridge, all simulations of reality. Finally, a rainstorm began, and by the ferocious sound of it, Diana fully expected to get wet. She drew further into the shelter of Mr. Dean's arms, and he responded by putting an arm around her waist. But just as she had forgotten Lucius Boyle, forgotten everyone but Mr. Dean, Mr. Boyle finally succeeded in pushing his way through the crowds and his voice sounded gratingly from beside her.

"Cousin Diana, did the sound of the storm frighten you? You are welcome to take my arm, if so," he said, and Diana unconsciously moved even closer to Mr. Dean in her attempt to get away from Lucius Boyle. However, as if becoming aware that he was practically embracing her in public, Mr. Dean dropped his hand from her waist, and stepped between her and Lucius Boyle.

"I am Mrs. Boyle's escort, and she has the use of my arm, should she need it," Mr. Dean said, and Diana thrilled at his protective tone.

"Of course, I beg your pardon, sir," Lucius Boyle said, still with that fake smile. "Cousin Diana, I will call on you tomorrow," he told her. And then, finally, he took his leave of them.

The rest of the evening, without Mr. Boyle's annoying presence, proved to be as delightful as the start of it had been. They watched the fireworks, listened to music, and even danced one set, before Diana and her group finally left Vauxhall a little after midnight, before the crowd became too rowdy. (Though Diana suspected some of the other Ladies of the Registry weren't planning on leaving for hours.) Diana felt that Lady Gordon had also enjoyed herself, and when Diana asked her on the carriage ride home whether she was pleased she had come with them, she agreed that she was. And when Monsieur de la Tour saw Lady Gordon to her door and said he would do himself the honor of calling on her the next day, she nodded and smiled in reply.

Lady Regina and Diana, after arriving home and changing into their nightclothes, happily relived the evening for another hour, and when Diana woke up around seven, she was confused to find herself in Regina's bed, where she'd fallen asleep shortly after Regina had confirmed that there was no plant called *"Sonophorus japonica"* and had continued to expound on the intelligence and other sterling attributes of Lord Jerome until Diana had been overcome with drowsiness. Regina, on the other hand, had listened patiently to Diana's story of Mr. Dean's bravery in protecting her from Mr. Boyle, and only yawned once. Diana, tiptoeing out of the room to go back to her own to sleep for another few hours, resolved to let Regina talk about Lord Jerome as much as she wanted to over breakfast.

11

DIANA COULD NOT escape Lucius Boyle.

He was like some kind of perpetually bowing puppy, always dogging her heels and either unaware or unheeding of her attempts to discourage him.

If she and Regina went shopping on Bond Street, he was frequently waiting outside the door of whatever shop they'd entered, be it milliner or modiste, offering to carry their boxes and escort them home. If they went to a ball, he'd somehow have procured an invitation and would appear at Diana's side as soon as she entered the room, asking for multiple dances. (And even though the Ladies of the Registry had decreed it was permissible to refuse a dance partner, Diana found it difficult to deny one of her own relations.) He was often to be found in Lady Regina's drawing room as well, conveniently scheduling his calls to coincide with the entrance of other ladies and

gentlemen, so that Diana and Regina could not deny they
were "at home."

After one of these calls had concluded and all the visitors had left, Diana was surprised to hear Mr. Dean's voice
in the hallway.

"I seem to have lost my watch fob when I was just here.
No need to announce me, I'll explain to the ladies," she
heard him say to the footman who had opened the door at
his knock.

Lady Regina had gone upstairs already, but Diana was
standing at the window, staring out of it, and thinking
how frustrating it was to always be in the company of the
man you disliked rather than being in the sole company of
the man . . . well, that you *didn't* dislike.

She turned at Mr. Dean's entrance and was surprised
by how her heart leapt in her chest at the sight of him,
especially as she had only said goodbye to him a few minutes earlier. He looked pleased to see her as well, and she
reflected for a moment on how two men's smiles could evoke
such vastly different reactions. When Lucius Boyle smiled
at her she thought it a repellant thing; it never seemed to
reach his eyes, which were always darting around greed-
ily, like a snake's. But Mr. Dean's smile lit up his entire face.
His gaze never faltered but met hers steadily, and there
was warmth, tenderness, even affection, in its silvery depths.

She wondered what he saw in *her* eyes and if they betrayed her fondness for him. She had yet to acknowledge
that she felt so strongly about him, even to herself.

"I beg your pardon, Mrs. Boyle, for intruding on you once again, but I seem to have misplaced my fob." He was still standing in the doorway as he said this, where he could be heard very clearly by the servants.

"It is no intrusion at all, Mr. Dean, you are always welcome," Diana replied.

Mr. Dean stepped into the room, hesitated a moment, and then shut the door behind him. He did it very softly, but the sound of the door closing seemed to Diana to be unnaturally loud in the quiet room. Then he crossed quickly to her side.

"I must sincerely beg your pardon this time," he said in a lowered tone, "because I did not, in truth, lose my fob. I placed it in the seat cushions myself so that I would have an excuse to come and speak with you after the others had left."

"It is no matter, Mr. Dean, I suspected it was an excuse," Diana replied, in a similarly quiet tone so as not to be overheard by the servants. She was as affected by his nearness as she always was, however, so was slightly breathless and doubted she could raise her voice much louder, anyway. She stepped back a few paces in an attempt to gather her composure before smiling playfully at him. "To be entirely honest with you, I didn't believe in the fob's existence, and am amazed you had the presence of mind to actually hide something."

He smiled briefly, but then quickly turned and walked to the sofa. She wondered if she had offended him when she had moved away from him, but then she realized he was feeling around between the cushions, looking for his fob. She followed him to the sofa, curious to see it, as she was aware he wore something hanging from his watch chain but had never paid it much notice. He retrieved it from the sofa just as she arrived at his side.

"May we sit?" he asked, and she was embarrassed that she hadn't already invited him to do so. But after she'd sat on the sofa and he sat next to her, she was conscious once again that they were in the room alone together, unchaperoned, with the door closed. She had only ever been in private like this with one other man, her late husband, and then only rarely, as they'd almost always been accompanied by Mildred.

Mr. Dean started to put the fob back on its chain but she stopped him. "May I see it?" she asked, reaching out her hand.

He placed the small golden object on her outstretched palm, his fingers lightly brushing her hand.

She stared unseeingly at the fob for a moment, forgetting it altogether in the excitement and nervousness she felt at his touch. She realized that her hand was trembling and was mortified that he might notice. Finally, when she'd calmed herself and her hand was steady, she brought the fob close and examined it carefully.

It was shaped like an upside-down V and carved from two shades of gold, rose and yellow, with bands of intertwining leaves and roses forming the neck of it, and ending at a round amethyst base. The base was an intaglio on which was inscribed the French phrase: *"Je pense à vous toi."*

"'I think of you,'" Diana murmured, translating the phrase aloud. But before she had finished her inspection, Mr. Dean had rushed into speech.

"I suppose it's not a *manly* trinket, but I'm very fond of it. My brother has one with the family crest; it's quite intimidating with a lion and armor and an obscure Latin motto, so my mother had this one made for me. She didn't want me to feel left out, I imagine." He spoke jerkily, almost as if he was embarrassed, and Diana realized the fob must mean a great deal to him. "I always thought I would give it to my wife one day to wear on a neck chain. If I marry, that is. And if she wanted it, of course. I suppose it's not very impressive, compared to a necklace of diamonds or sapphires."

"It's beautiful. I'm sure she would greatly cherish such a gift," Diana said, wondering why Mr. Dean was so self-conscious, and if it was because he was worried she would find his treasured possession lacking. Or perhaps it was because he was not wealthy and couldn't afford to buy a woman expensive gifts, and knew that Diana *did* have the means to buy precious gemstones and it made him feel inferior. Diana remembered very clearly how it felt to be poor, and how, though she'd have given her mother the world if she could have, the only gifts she'd been able to give her were drawings she'd made on scraps of paper, or little baubles made over from other people's garbage. "*I would cherish such a gift,*" Diana emphatically said, and so eager was she to reassure him that she did not think how her words could be misinterpreted. However, when Mr. Dean's expression changed to one of delighted wonder, and he moved closer and grasped her shoulders, she realized that he had imbued more significance into her statement than she'd intended. "I mean, that is—I didn't mean—" she said inarticulately, too nervous to form a complete sentence.

She was dismayed to see his face fall, and he dropped his hands from her shoulders as if scalded. "I apologize," he said, backing away from her.

"You need not—" she began, but he wouldn't allow her to absolve him.

"You have made it clear that you have no desire to marry," he said, "and I have no right to press my attentions on you." He moved further away from her as he said this, and Diana shivered a little in an involuntary response.

"It was my fault entirely—" Diana said, but once again he interrupted, and she realized he was indeed upset, as he was usually scrupulously polite when conversing with her.

"No, I wronged you before we even met, publishing that directory and exposing you to attentions that are burdensome to you. I've regretted it many times since, but I don't think I fully appreciated the enormity of my mistake until very recently," he said. "That is the reason why I manufactured this opportunity to speak to you alone. I wanted to talk to you about Lucius Boyle."

Diana wasn't sure she was ready to change topics so quickly. Her head was still whirling from Mr. Dean's near-embrace, and at the present moment she wasn't as convinced she wanted a life of chaste singleness as she had been when she'd first met him. "You wanted to talk to me about Lucius Boyle?" she repeated, as she could only barely comprehend what he was saying and wanted to confirm she'd heard him correctly. She'd had no idea what he had intended to discuss when he'd created this opportunity to be alone with her, but if she were to have her pick of subjects, Lucius Boyle would not be one of them.

"I feel it is my fault that he is so determinedly pursuing you, since my directory is inevitably what brought you to his notice, and I wanted to be sure I was correct in assuming you did not desire his attentions before I rid you of them."

"Before you . . . rid me of them?" Diana asked, thinking as she did so that he must think her simpleminded, to keep repeating his words as she did.

"I beg your pardon, that sounded as if I intended to murder him," said Mr. Dean, with a crooked smile. "I don't intend anything so drastic. But before I do anything at all, I wanted to obtain your permission."

"This is very chivalrous of you, Mr. Dean, but you are mistaken in thinking that it is your fault my cousin is pursuing me. It was my sister-in-law who introduced him to me and who is promoting the match."

"Is she? That's interesting," Mr. Dean said, frowning slightly.

"Therefore, as eager as I am to escape Mr. Boyle's attentions, I could not impose on you in such a manner," Diana said, though she couldn't help but feel a thrill of excitement that he wanted to intervene on her behalf. She had used the word "chivalrous" without giving it much thought, but she did feel a little like a maiden in the Middle Ages, with a brave knight offering to joust for her favor.

"Nonsense, it is what any man of honor would do if he became aware of a lady in distress," Mr. Dean said. "It is not an imposition in the least; it is my privilege."

Diana decided not to waste any more time trying to dissuade him from helping her, for if he considered such a thing a *privilege*, it would be selfish of her to deprive him of it. And, as independent as she liked to think herself, and as happy as she was to have total authority at Whitley House and not have to answer to any man, she had to admit it was refreshing to have someone constitute himself her protector and defender. It occurred to her that perhaps this was what a real marriage was like, and how a true husband should act. Maybe Lady Gordon was correct: it wasn't matrimony itself that was so terrible but entering into it with the wrong person.

"Well, sir, if you are determined to help me, I will admit to you, in confidence, that I find Mr. Boyle's suit unwelcome. But it's difficult for me to dissuade him as he is a relation, however distant," Diana said. "If you are able to find a way to spare me his attentions, you would have my heartfelt gratitude."

"That is more than I could wish for," Mr. Dean said, with a slight bow, and Diana felt none of the irritation that Mr. Boyle's bows induced in her. In fact, when Mr. Dean lowered his head, it made her conscious of the fact that his face was now closer to her own. As were his lips . . .

After a silence that stretched a little too long, Diana realized she had been gazing at him, at his mouth in particular, and quickly looked down at her hands. Only to see that she was still clasping his fob.

"Oh, Mr. Dean, I beg your pardon; I never returned this to you," she said, and in her eagerness to do so she dropped it just shy of the hand he'd reached out. "Oh! I am so sorry," she said, looking down to where the fob lay glittering on the carpet. She dropped to the floor to retrieve it as Mr. Dean was telling her there was no harm done and he would get it. But by this time she already had the fob in her hand and had begun rising from the floor just as he was kneeling down. She accidentally collided into him and her head brushed against his chest.

And stayed there.

Diana could not figure out what had happened, she just knew that when she attempted to pull her head away from Mr. Dean's chest she could not, and such an action caused a painful jerking of her hair. She felt exceedingly awkward and uncomfortable, especially as she was in a precarious position and had to hold on to his arm so that she did not fall.

"Mrs. Boyle, I'm afraid that your hair has caught on my watch chain. Or perhaps it's stuck on my button, I cannot exactly tell," Mr. Dean said, and although Diana could not see his face, she imagined he must feel as silly and awkward as she did. Though perhaps not. She was the one plastered against his chest, practically embracing him, while in a crouching position *on the floor*. Why had she ever thought it a good idea to get on the floor? She had not spent very long at that school when she was fourteen, but she could imagine that one of the cardinal rules must have been: "Proper young ladies should never crouch down on drawing room floors." Was it all a bad dream? She did not see how it could really be happening. She closed her eyes, hoping that when she opened them, she'd wake up alone in her bed, but she could still *smell* Mr. Dean, so she knew she was not dreaming. She was thankful that he, like Beau Brummel, obviously believed in the importance of daily bathing and freshly laundered clothes. His scent was not at all offensive, quite the opposite in fact. It was rather enticing, like the man himself. But such thoughts were not at all helpful in her current predicament. She tried to pull her head away again, but only succeeded in jerking her hair so hard her eyes watered.

Mr. Dean put his hand against the back of her head to

keep her from moving it. "Please, don't. You'll only do yourself an injury. I can free you, if you will allow me?"

"Yes, of course," she said, even though she had no idea what his methods would entail. She hoped they did not involve sharp blades, but then again, a haircut might be the quickest and least painful way out of this.

"If you would just make yourself comfortable, this might take a few minutes," Mr. Dean said, and she could feel the reverberation of the words in his chest as he spoke. She wondered how he could think she could possibly ever be *comfortable* in such a situation, but he slowly shifted his own position while gently guiding her with his hands, and somehow he was sitting on the floor and she was perched on his thigh with her legs stretched out in front of her, and it was definitely less awkward than the bent position they'd been in previously, though she was still overcome with embarrassment to find herself in such an intimate situation. Then she felt his fingers gently moving through her hair, and it was as if a host of butterflies were fluttering inside of her.

"I am more sorry than I can say to have to take such liberties," Mr. Dean said, in a constricted tone, and she wondered if his entire body was tingling from head to toe, as hers was. "I cannot see what I'm doing, but I am trying to be as gentle as possible."

"Don't worry, I'm fine," she managed to respond, which was possibly the biggest untruth she had ever told.

He removed a few hairpins, then threaded his fingers through the strands he'd released, and Diana hoped he couldn't feel how rapidly her heart was beating. "Your hair is like silk; it's so beautiful," he whispered, as if he did not mean to say it aloud but could not stop himself.

"Thank you," Diana whispered back, settling herself more securely onto his lap and into his arms. She had nearly forgotten what had brought her to this moment with its attendant embarrassment, and now, instead of wanting it to end, she was wishing she could stay forever in this haven of warmth and tenderness. Though if she were perfectly honest with herself, his arms weren't exactly a safe haven, as there was a very real danger in the desire that was stirring between them.

Mr. Dean had at least retained enough presence of mind to continue his task because, although Diana had lost almost all awareness of her surroundings, if he did not free her from her entanglement their only alternatives were to be discovered together or to call for help, either of which might prove disastrous to her reputation. However, he did not seem to be in a hurry, and removed all of her pins until the hair that wasn't caught in his watch chain was tumbling down around her shoulders. Then he proceeded to run his hands through waves and curls that Diana knew, and he had to have known, too, were not part of the problem.

Still, she did not utter one word of protest, even when his fingers dipped down to caress her neck, which made it more than obvious he'd lost sight of his supposed goal. But finally, inevitably, he returned to his task, making little murmured apologies when he felt he'd tugged too hard in his attempts to free her.

Diana would murmur reassurances back, though she had little idea what she was saying, and when he finally succeeded in detaching her hair, she made no move to remove herself from his arms. But really, she hadn't much time to do so, because as soon as she raised her head from his chest he was kissing her.

His hands were still in her hair and so she figured that gave her the right to touch his, too, and she understood then why he had so enjoyed stroking hers. She wanted to tell him she found his hair beautiful as well, but not only was she unsure if that was the type of compliment you paid a man, it would also require her to stop kissing him, which she was extremely loath to do.

She was not sure how long or how many times he had kissed her, she was not even sure how (or if) you were supposed to keep count of such a thing, she only knew it seemed not nearly long enough when she heard the creak of the stairs.

She was aware of the noise before Mr. Dean was, and when she pulled away from him, he merely looked confused, as if he hadn't quite awakened from a dream. "Someone is coming," Diana hissed at him, and his rapturous look quickly transformed to one of alertness, then trepidation.

They both jumped up from the floor and Diana noticed that she must have dropped the fob at some point during their embrace, as it was lying, forgotten, on the carpet. Diana allowed Mr. Dean to retrieve it, having learned her lesson. He quickly put the fob in his pocket, before picking up her hairpins, which were also scattered on the floor.

"Mrs. Boyle, please forgive me," he said, handing her the pins with a look of dismay. "Your hair . . . this all looks extremely untoward . . ." he said, running his hand through his own hair. This prompted Diana to try to tidy hers as well, but she could tell from Mr. Dean's expression that such efforts were useless; there was absolutely no way she could pin it back up before they were discovered. And a lady with her hair down, alone, in the presence of a man she was not married to, was breaking a number of rules so shocking that even the Ladies of the Registry could not absolve her of the consequences.

They could now hear voices in the hall, and Diana was relieved when she realized that it was Regina talking to a servant. Perhaps she was leaving on an errand and would not even enter the room.

This wish was not to be granted, however. Diana and Mr. Dean stared at each other in silence, their eyes wide, as they heard Regina say: "Mr. Dean is here?" and then an apparently affirmative reply from the footman, whose words were indecipherable. They then heard Regina's footsteps as she approached the door, and they both turned to watch fearfully as the knob turned, the door opened, and Regina entered the room.

"Good afternoon, Mr. Dean," Regina said with a pleasant smile, which disappeared after she had fully taken in the scene before her. Diana realized it must look very bad, indeed, if Regina could look so very shocked at the mere sight of her. Regina turned quickly and shut the door behind her, though after doing so, she said loudly, "I've been told you misplaced your fob."

Regina then walked over to where Diana and Mr. Dean stood. "Diana, are you all right?" she asked.

"I am fine, Regina, though I realize I do not look it," Diana said, with a slight smile.

Regina expelled a breath of relief and said, "Well, I, more than anyone, should know not to judge by appearances. Perhaps I am *de trop* and should leave you to your private affair—matters?" she asked, deciding to rephrase the sentence but doing so a little too late.

"Of course you are not *de trop*, it is merely a comedy of errors," Diana said, at the same time Mr. Dean said, "I hold myself fully to blame, Lady Regina."

Diana turned to him and said, "No one is to blame, Mr. Dean." She then turned back to address Regina. "Though if someone is at fault it is I, for being so clumsy as to drop Mr. Dean's fob after finding it, bumping into him when we both bent down to retrieve it, and getting my hair caught in his watch chain."

Regina laughed. "Is that what happened to your hair?

You look like you've been dragged through a hedgerow. And did you lose all your pins in the process, too?"

Diana could not control her blush at her friend's innocent question, and Mr. Dean also looked uncomfortable. "It was a difficult task, extricating ourselves. I had to . . . remove Mrs. Boyle's, um, hairpins," he said, looking so very guilt-stricken that Diana reflected that he must be as unused to participating in amorous intrigues as she was. (A thought which delighted her for some reason that she didn't have time to analyze at that moment.)

"I see," said Regina, and Diana was very much afraid that she did. There was an awkward silence, broken at last by Mr. Dean.

"If Lady Regina will help you with your hair, Mrs. Boyle, I will take my leave of you. But I will keep you apprised of my progress in that matter we discussed earlier."

"I greatly appreciate your assistance, but I wish you will not go to *too* much trouble," Diana said, realizing he spoke of Lucius Boyle.

"It is no trouble at all," he said softly, and taking her hand in his, he bowed over it, before saying goodbye to Lady Regina and leaving the room.

"'A comedy of errors,' was it?" Lady Regina asked. "Were you enacting a scene from *A Midsummer Night's Dream?*"

Diana ignored her friend's remark, plopping herself down on the sofa with a sigh. "*Can* you do anything with my hair? I would prefer that none of the servants see me coming out of the room like this."

"I would do a very poor job of it I'm afraid, but if you give me your pins, I think I can manage a coronet of braids. And if any of the servants notice, we can pretend we were trying out new hairstyles on each other. Perhaps you should do something to my hair as well," Regina said. "We can tell them it's a new parlor game that's all the rage."

Regina started braiding Diana's hair, but there was a definite feeling of constraint between them. "What I told you was the truth, by the way," Diana finally said, in an attempt to dispel the uneasy atmosphere. "I did get my hair caught in his watch chain in the manner I described. But it's not the entire truth. While he was untangling my hair we were thrown into very close proximity, practically an embrace. And after I was finally free, he, that is, we . . . did embrace."

"That was rather obvious, Diana dear. You both looked entirely too guilty, like cats who had just been feasting on some particularly tasty cream. And it was mighty suspicious that he found it necessary to remove every last one of your hairpins. Though better those than any items of clothing, I suppose."

"Regina, really! It was just a kiss," Diana said, shocked.

"Only one?"

"Regina!" Diana said, before she started giggling. She was suddenly overcome with a rush of gratitude that she had a friend in whom she could confide, and one, too, who wouldn't immediately assume the worst of her. She hugged Regina, startling her. "Thank you."

"I am not sure what you are thanking me for, but if it's for your new coiffure, I'm not quite done with it," Regina said, returning her hug. "And you haven't seen it yet."

Diana laughed and was silent once again. Regina broke the silence after a minute or two to tell her she had finished and it was Diana's turn to do *her* hair. "And Diana?" Regina said.

"Yes?"

"I just wondered, couldn't Mr. Dean have just removed his chain from his waistcoat, and freed you much more quickly?"

Diana thought about it for a moment and then shrugged. "I am not sure. Possibly. Neither of us were thinking very clearly. But I am very glad he did not," she said, with a reminiscent smile.

12

MAXWELL LEFT LADY Regina's townhome in a daze, barely aware of where he was walking. At first he felt a sense of wonder, elation, ecstasy; there did not seem to be an adequate word to describe his feelings. He had held Mrs. Boyle, *Diana*, in his arms. He had run his fingers through that cloud of silky dark hair and kissed those delectable lips. He had caressed the soft skin at the nape of her neck, its petallike smoothness a sensuous contrast to his calloused fingertips. He realized suddenly that he was trembling, and flopped down onto the front step of the nearest townhouse without first checking it for dirt, uncaring whether he muddied his buff-colored inexpressibles.

But he could not relive that wondrous experience for too long before his conscience began to plague him. He had taken shocking liberties with a lady of his acquaintance. As a gentleman his course was clear: he was obligated to make her an offer of marriage. Of course, it was not merely an obligation but, he suddenly realized, his greatest desire; he wanted Diana like he'd never wanted anything or anyone in his life. Not just in his arms but at his side, always, as the marriage vow said: "For better for worse, for richer for poorer, in sickness and in health." He could not envision his days without her in them; it would be like a world with no light. Whatever feeling of interest, attraction, or fondness he had once felt for his sister-in-law was nothing compared to what he felt now, for Diana. He said aloud, "I love her. I love Diana," and smiled at the sound of the most beautiful sentence he had ever heard.

However, his smile quickly faded when he remembered that Diana had made it very clear that she had no interest in marriage. And even if she did change her mind, she would never consider an offer of marriage from him, Maxwell Dean, author of a directory where he had listed her as a *commodity*! He groaned aloud, cringing at the very thought. Coming to know and love Diana had brought him to a fuller realization of the wrongness of his actions, and the weight of his offense felt as if it was suffocating him. He ran a finger around the neck of his cravat, attempting to loosen it so he could take a deeper breath.

He realized now that his humiliating rejection by his sister-in-law had colored his views of courtship and marriage. He had thought of marriage primarily in practical terms; that matches should be made based on this person's assets and that person's deficits. But his feelings had completely changed, and now he would not care if Diana hadn't a penny to her name; in fact, he wished that she did not! How was she ever to believe in his love for her, when he had demonstrated himself to be one of those lowest, most despicable of creatures, a fortune hunter?

Max heard the townhouse door opening and jumped to his feet, walking hurriedly away. He had no desire to see or talk to anyone. He turned down a side street, one where he was less likely to encounter anyone he knew, taking a circuitous route home while he pondered the situation. He knew it would be useless to propose and would probably do more harm than good, as Diana would assume him to be motivated by either duty or money and would be even less inclined to believe he loved her. And since she would most likely refuse him, it would make subsequent meetings between them awkward. She might even avoid him altogether, which would be the worst possible outcome. So, as much as it went against his principles as a gentleman *not* to do the honorable thing and propose, he decided it would be best to wait until he had proven his love for her.

But how was he to do that? He considered what he knew about love, and realized he knew very little. He supposed his parents were fond of each other, and if prodded they might admit to mutual esteem, but he did not think the word "love" was part of their vocabulary. (Maxwell's nanny, on the other hand, had called him "love" from the time he was born. He had actually believed that to be his name and only discovered his error at the age of four when he'd attempted to correct his mother when she'd called him Maxwell.) But while his nanny was of a more affectionate temperament than his mother, she was no example of connubial bliss, either; she had been married to a gruff blacksmith and had taken the position as nanny in order to get away from her husband.

Nor did he consider the fabled lovers from literature appropriate examples, as their stories were quite depressing, and they inevitably had a tragic end. He could not remember any that were happily married. Of the three couples who immediately sprang to mind—Lancelot and Guinevere, Tristan and Isolde, and Romeo and Juliet—the last were the only ones not married to other people, and they had killed themselves!

London society had very few happy marriages for him to study; Lord and Lady Gordon being one of the only couples he knew who'd been faithful to each other, and Lord Gordon could no longer be approached for advice. And he did not think he was brave enough to speak to Lady Gordon; he doubted she would consider him a worthy suitor for her friend.

Maxwell finally decided that, since it was unlikely that he could ever convince Diana of his love with mere words, he would take the phrase "Actions are more significant than words" as his maxim. His determination to assist her in her present difficulties might be the most effective way of proving his love. He hated seeing Diana subjected to the attentions of that jackass Lucius Boyle, whose pursuit amounted to little more than persecution, and Maxwell genuinely wanted to help Diana escape Lucius, whether it forwarded his own suit or not. He wondered if he'd somehow stumbled across the real meaning of love: wanting another's happiness more than your own.

Maxwell was so suspicious of Lucius Boyle, he did not believe that was even his name. Apparently someone of that name did exist, as Mildred Boyle had known him when he was a child, but who was to say this so-called Lucius Boyle was that person? It was very easy to say you were a man who had emigrated to the other side of the world more than a decade ago and had never been seen since. Maxwell had attempted to talk to him about America, and it seemed to Maxwell that Lucius knew less about the continent than Maxwell did. When asked where he'd lived after emigrating, Lucius had answered "Boston," but then when Maxwell mentioned he had a friend who lived in Boston, Lucius immediately said he'd most recently lived outside of Boston, in Baltimore. Maxwell had later checked a map of America and Baltimore was nowhere near Boston. Of course, his words could be interpreted in different ways, but his very demeanor when he and Maxwell were talking had been suspicious. It was obvious he did not want to talk about his supposed sojourn in America, and he had changed the subject as quickly as possible. Had anyone else even questioned his bona fides? The only person who might possibly do so was Mildred, and she seemed so eager to promote this match that her own motives were in question. Could she be in league with the soi-disant Lucius Boyle? Or, if he was an impostor, had Mildred been tricked into accepting him?

Of course, the man could be who he claimed to be, as well as a scoundrel and avaricious fortune hunter. But Maxwell felt there had to be something he was trying to hide, as he seemed so very inauthentic, as if he was always playing a role.

He was glad that Diana hadn't rejected Lucius Boyle outright, but still danced with him and seemingly accepted his attentions. Maxwell thought Diana had successfully hidden her feelings from Lucius, who was not the most perceptive of men, even though Maxwell, who was very perceptive where Diana was concerned, had discerned immediately that she disliked Lucius. Maxwell didn't want Diana to reject him too quickly, however, because a man faced with the rejection of his suit and the loss of a potential fortune could grow desperate, and there were many cases where such men had abducted heiresses in an effort to force them into marriage. Though some of these women had later been rescued from their abductors, one could only imagine the horrors they had suffered in the meantime. Maxwell, thinking of Diana suffering such things, was sickened by the thought, and had to force himself not to think of it. Especially as it made him feel even worse about having inadvertently exposed the ladies in the directory to such dangers.

Therefore Maxwell, who would have preferred to spend more time dwelling on his ladylove and her many charms, told himself he must instead concentrate on the mystery of her unwanted suitor and rid her of his attentions as he had promised. Though he'd just scoffed at romantic stories of old, he suddenly felt himself akin to a medieval knight on a chivalrous quest: he would pledge himself to his lady's service and perform this task with no personal reward as his object but instead find fulfillment in a courtly love; one which existed on a higher, spiritual plane and was entirely unselfish.

However, if Diana found herself so delighted with his efforts on her behalf that she insisted on rewarding him, perhaps with another one (or more) of those intoxicating kisses, well, he wouldn't be so selfish as to deny her.

THE INVESTIGATION INTO Lucius Boyle's origins began the next day, when Maxwell questioned Diana during a morning call, from which Boyle was thankfully absent. This was the first time Max and Diana had seen each other since their embrace, and they were both initially a little shy and self-conscious, but Lord Jerome soon arrived and began speaking to Lady Regina, and that couple's light-hearted talk helped alleviate some of the tension in the room.

"I believe you said that Miss Boyle claims Lucius as her nephew?" Maxwell asked Diana, after Jerome and Regina had begun a private conversation of their own.

"Yes, that is what Mildred told me. And Lucius Boyle refers to her as 'Aunt' Mildred."

"Then he would have to be the son of her deceased brother, or his surname would not be Boyle. Were you acquainted with your brother-in-law before his death?" Maxwell asked.

"No, I never knew him," Diana said slowly, her brow furrowed. "Actually, now that you mention it, it's very strange; I had never heard Mildred or Mr. Boyle ever mention a brother before Mildred introduced Lucius to me."

"Do the Boyles possess a family Bible that might contain information about this mysterious brother?" Maxwell asked.

"Yes, at Whitley House there is one."

"Could we go look at it?" Mr. Dean asked.

"What, now?" Diana asked, surprised.

"It's a nice day for a drive," Mr. Dean said.

Diana looked pointedly at the window, where rain trickled down the panes. "It looks rather wet to me. We could just ask Lucius Boyle. If he doesn't call today, I'm sure he'll be here tomorrow or the next. Unfortunately," Diana said, with a sigh.

"I'd prefer not to ask him, if you don't mind. I don't want him to know that we are looking into his background."

"I understand. But I should probably write to Mildred and let her know that I am coming to Whitley House," Diana said slowly, thinking aloud.

There was a lull in the other couple's conversation, and Regina, who had overheard the last part of Diana and Maxwell's discussion, asked Diana if she was thinking of visiting her home.

"Yes," Diana answered. "Perhaps tomorrow."

"May I come along?" Regina asked. "It would be nice to take a little break from London, and I'm very curious about Whitley House, as well."

"It's a very nice house," Lord Jerome said, and Regina's smile faltered for a moment. She had apparently forgotten that Jerome had once called on Diana and she was not pleased at the reminder.

"You are both welcome to join us," Diana said, anxious to reassure Regina that there was nothing, and never had been anything, between her and Lord Jerome. "I don't think I was very cordial to you on your first visit to Whitley House, Lord Jerome."

"It was my fault entirely," Jerome said. "You weren't expecting callers and were more than gracious, under the circumstances."

"Didn't Raymond Pryce call on you as well?" Lady Regina asked Diana, having regained her savoir faire. "I would have liked to have been there to witness *that*."

"It was extremely awkward, as I recall," Lord Jerome said. "Mr. Pryce surmised that Mrs. Boyle, an 'ace of spades,' had 'whiddled our scrap' and encouraged me to cast my line 'where the fish are biting,'" he quoted, straight-faced, and the words sounded even more ludicrous said in Lord Jerome's very proper Eton College accent.

"I don't even know what most of that means, but unfortunately I can guess," said Diana, who could now laugh at something that had not seemed funny at all at the time.

"It is settled then?" Regina asked, taking charge as usual. "We will go to Twickenham tomorrow?"

"I suppose so," Diana said, with an inquiring look at Mr. Dean, who nodded, and said he would hire a carriage for the trip. "I don't know why I feel so reluctant," Diana said, with a sigh. "But I do not look forward to seeing Mildred or Lucius."

"Maybe we'll be fortunate and she'll have gone out," Regina said.

"Mildred never goes anywhere. But I suppose there is no need to inform her of my intentions. It is my house, after all," Diana said, assuming a confident demeanor and hoping that it would actually give her confidence.

Mr. Dean, who was the instigator of the visit to Whitley House, now had very little to say on the subject, and after Regina and Jerome had returned to their private conversation, Diana looked at Maxwell, her eyebrows raised. "Aren't you pleased that we will be going to Whitley House tomorrow, as you wished?"

"Yes, of course," he said, although his tone and frown said the opposite. He had just been reminded that Diana had been pursued for her house, thanks to his publication of the directory, and now wished he had not suggested going there. He did not want her to think he was looking it over, as a potential prize if he should succeed in winning her hand. But then he reminded himself that his motives were entirely altruistic. "I *am* pleased to be going to your home, but I look on it primarily as a means to an end, not necessarily a pleasure jaunt," he explained. "It's a good place to begin our search for information about Lucius Boyle."

"Do you suspect he is not who he claims to be?" Diana asked.

"Possibly. What do you think?"

"I have no idea. I do find *something* suspicious about him; I've felt an instinctive distrust of him since we first met but, then again, some of his mannerisms do put me in mind of Mildred and her brother, my late husband."

"Well then, perhaps this trip is a waste of time," Mr. Dean said, slightly discouraged that his theory might prove to be wrong.

"Or perhaps we can find some enjoyment from it," Diana said, with a teasing smile.

"Since I will be in your company, nothing is more certain," Mr. Dean said, returning her smile.

13

Diana was eating her toast and marmalade in the breakfast room the next morning when Regina entered, carrying the silver salver from the hall. It was conspicuously empty.

"Diana, you did not remove any cards from the hall tray, did you?"

"I did not."

"How very odd," Regina said, setting the tray down before pouring herself a cup of tea and joining Diana at the table. "Have you noticed that we have not been receiving as many invitations recently?"

"Frankly, I was glad to have a respite. It felt like we were burning the candle at both ends for a few weeks," Diana said. "But now that you mention it, there do seem to be fewer invitations of late."

"And many of the ladies who had been calling on us have not been to call in over a week, at least," Regina said, frowning. "And they appear to have developed very poor eyesight as well. When I nodded to Lady Jersey when I passed her in the park a few days ago, she did not even acknowledge me."

"Yes, I noticed something similar but I hoped I was mistaken," Diana said. "Lady Gordon still calls very regularly, and we see Miss Jarmyn often as well. And what reason could the ladies have for avoiding us? It makes no sense. We've all been very busy since Vauxhall, and they may just be tied up with their own affairs."

Regina seemed to accept this reply, but Diana knew that despite her friend's prior boasting about not caring whether she was accepted by London society or not, she was still very sensitive to slights such as these. Diana had never aspired to be part of society; hers was no more than a genteel family with no connection to the nobility. But Regina was of noble birth, the daughter of a marquess, and this entitled her to a position in the society that had shunned her. Diana also knew Regina to have been wounded by her previous rejection, whatever she might say otherwise, and that she had delighted in being accepted and included once again.

Not only that, but it was Regina who had founded their group; hers was the idea behind the grand ball that had resulted in society clasping all of them to their collective bosoms, and if the other women had now forgotten her, and might even be purposely excluding her, it was an undeserved and hurtful snub.

However, Diana greatly hoped that they were both mistaken, and that it was all a coincidence, or, at worst, an easily resolved misunderstanding.

They had the answer less than an hour later, when Lady Gordon came to call. This was surprising in itself, as it was much earlier than the time for traditional "morning" calls, which typically occurred in the afternoon.

Lady Gordon said as much when they joined her in the drawing room. "I beg your pardon for calling so early, but I needed to speak to you in private, before any other callers arrive."

"*If* any other callers arrive," Regina said, with a twisted smile.

"What, has no one been calling?" Lady Gordon asked, looking concerned.

"Just the usual: Mr. Dean, Lord Jerome, Mr. Boyle, and sundry other impoverished gents," Regina said lightly, as if it was not a matter of great concern to her.

"No ladies have been to call?" Lady Gordon asked.

"Miss Jarmyn has come a few times with Mr. Pryce," Diana said, but Lady Gordon waved a dismissive hand as if Miss Jarmyn was of no importance. And Diana supposed that from society's viewpoint, she wasn't.

"That jealous cat," Lady Gordon said vehemently.

"Miss Jarmyn?" Diana asked, surprised and a little disappointed. She liked Miss Jarmyn and did not think it was kind of Lady Gordon to disparage her.

"No, definitely *not* Miss Jarmyn. I am very pleased to

hear that she, at least, has the courage to stand by you all," Lady Gordon said, to Diana's relief. "No, I'm referring to Lady Jersey. She has decreed Lady Regina, and you as well, Diana, by virtue of your association with Regina, unwelcome in London society. She has rehashed that old elopement scandal and claimed that Regina is attempting to buy her way back into favor by means of her fortune. Sally Jersey, of all people! The richest woman in England! And one who has made very obvious her disregard for the marriage bond. But she cannot bear it that when Regina entertained, it drew guests away from her stuffy old Almack's assemblies, and that Regina's favor was being courted as much or more than hers. Also, when Regina rewrote some of the rules of society for our ball, that was a slap in the face to Sally, who considers herself its queen."

"We should have listened to you when you advised us not to hold the Vauxhall excursion on a Wednesday," Diana said worriedly. "I didn't think it would matter to anyone what we did, and it was so difficult finding an available evening, but Miss Ballard had two of London's most eligible bachelors escorting her there instead of Almack's, which I'm sure also enraged Lady Jersey."

Lady Gordon nodded her agreement with Diana's statement before sitting down next to Regina on the sofa and taking her hand. "I'm more sorry than I can say, my dear. I know this is a painful reminder of your past mistreatment. I wish I could do something, but I haven't the influence she has."

Regina smiled bravely. "Thank you for your concern, Lady Gordon, but it does not matter. As you are aware, I survived once, and I will survive again—" But her voice began to wobble and her face crumpled, before she dropped her face into her hands to hide it.

Lady Gordon pulled her into her arms, patting her shoulder, which caused the tears Regina had been restraining to trickle forth. Diana's own eyes welled up; she hated seeing her friend's distress. She also felt some of Regina's pain. Now that she knew, for a fact, that the ladies were snubbing them, it felt like the worst kind of betrayal.

"Are the Ladies of the Registry still calling on *you*?" Diana asked Lady Gordon. "After all, everyone has been so busy, we haven't had one of our meetings in weeks."

"That is true," Lady Gordon said. "I don't think any of us anticipated how hectic the social whirl would become. I've been going out more often myself. Perhaps we're leaping to conclusions about *them*, at least. I will invite them to call upon me, and we shall see."

Regina had stopped crying and pulled away from Lady Gordon. She blew her nose in a handkerchief and attempted other repairs to her appearance before smiling at her two friends. "Dear Lady Gordon," she said, squeezing that lady's hand. "I apologize for being so poor-spirited and weeping upon your shoulder like the heroine of a tragic novel."

"Nonsense, you had good reason to be upset and I was happy my shoulder could be of service to you," Lady Gordon replied bracingly. "Though I imagine Lord Jerome's shoulder would have been even more to your liking."

Regina laughed and denied that she'd found Lady Gordon's shoulder lacking in any way. Diana was surprised Lady Gordon would tease Regina about Jerome; it seemed out of character for the dignified widow, but Diana soon realized it was done partly as an attempt to distract Regina from her troubles. This was confirmed when Lady Gordon winked at Diana behind Regina's back.

Soon after Lady Gordon took her leave, the ladies received an unexpected call from the very man Lady Gordon had just mentioned.

The fact that Lord Jerome had called wasn't surprising; he was a regular caller and both ladies saw him frequently. Especially Regina, who had seen him more times in the last two months than she had the entire two years of their engagement. But it was midmorning, and still earlier for a call than was strictly polite.

"Perhaps it's a good thing we had no invitations last night, since this morning is proving to be so busy," Regina said to Diana, upon hearing the arrival of another caller. When Lord Jerome entered the room, his eyes flew to Lady Regina's with such a look of concern that Diana was surprised. She'd never seen the highly polished Lord Jerome appear so agitated.

"Mrs. Boyle," he said with a bow. "I apologize for calling at such an early hour, but I would appreciate a word with Lady Regina in private."

Diana had started walking toward the door before he'd even finished his sentence, having already realized her presence was unwelcome. After Diana left the room, Regina, who had not quite recovered from her last visitor, attempted to assume her usual insouciant demeanor.

"Jerome, this is unexpected. Please, take a seat. Have you breakfasted? Would you like anything?" Regina asked him, but her voice quavered a little when she met his intense gaze.

He ignored her question, striding over to the sofa and sitting close beside her. "Regina, I am sorry to have to be the one to tell you this, but there is a rumor—"

Regina interrupted him. "If this is about Lady Jersey's pronouncement that I am no longer welcome in polite society, I already know. Lady Gordon was just here."

"Lady Gordon? She is willing to stand by you against Lady Jersey?"

"Yes, she has proven to be a true friend," Regina said, with a fond smile.

"A better friend than I was to you," Jerome said bitterly. "It never occurred to me at the time, but if I'd stood by you publicly after your failed elopement, you might not have been ostracized in the first place."

"That is very gentlemanly of you, and I very much appreciate the sentiment, but you are entirely blameless in that affair. I had already written to you that our engagement was at an end; I had no claim on you at all."

"We had been friends, though, even if we were no longer betrothed," Jerome said.

"It's true that I thought of *you* as a friend, but I know you just thought of me as an annoying younger sister," Regina said with a self-deprecating smile.

"Is that what you believed? Is that why you ended the betrothal?" Jerome asked, his voice rising.

"Why, yes. I knew you had no romantic feelings for me, and then, when it appeared there was a gentleman who *did*—" Regina jumped up from the sofa and walked quickly to the window. Just speaking about that time caused a recurrence of her feelings of humiliation and worthlessness and she couldn't look Jerome in the eye. "I should have realized, however, that he didn't care for me, either. It appears my fortune is my only desirable trait," Regina said, in a tone of voice she tried very hard to make jovial, but instead sounded pathetic to her ears.

She heard Jerome come up behind her but she continued looking unseeingly out the window until he placed his hands on her shoulders and gently turned her to face him. "Regina, you are the most desirable woman I have ever known," he said, and in proof of his statement, the gaze that met hers was positively scorching. "When I learned that our parents had arranged our marriage, I couldn't believe my luck. But what kind of cad would I have been to have demonstrated my feelings to a girl of fifteen, or even sixteen? I was waiting for you to grow up. I was so proud of myself for my patience, which, I can assure you, is not an easy quality for a young man of nineteen or twenty to display. But as soon as you'd turned seventeen, when I was beginning to think you *were* old enough and I could finally show you my true feelings, you jilted me."

Regina was deeply moved by this confession, and was also shaken by the look in Jerome's eyes and his grasp on her shoulders. But she was determined not to make the same mistake she'd made at seventeen and be taken in by a fortune hunter. If she could just think clearly, she had this nagging feeling that there was something more that needed to be explained.

She took a few steps back, pulling out of his grasp, so that she could concentrate on her thoughts and not his touch. He obviously assumed this to be a rejection and his face fell, before he smiled in his usual satirical manner. "I beg your pardon for embarrassing you with this unwanted confession. It's apparent that you did not have similar feelings for me," he said.

"That's not true. I did care for you, very much. It's just, you so recently called on Mrs. Boyle, and I, I cannot bear to be made a fool of a second time . . ."

Jerome dropped the care-for-naught demeanor that Regina was beginning to realize he used to mask his true feelings, and his earnest expression returned. "Regina," he said, "had you never wondered why I didn't marry in the years since our betrothal ended? You were the only woman I'd ever considered marrying, and after you jilted me, I had no interest in marrying at all. It wasn't until you came back to live in London earlier this year and I saw you once again and you didn't even acknowledge me . . . I'm not sure if you recall; it was at the theatre, in March, before I'd even heard of that blasted directory. When you wouldn't speak to me, wouldn't even nod at me, well, it made me feel ridiculous that I'd let a boyhood infatuation with a woman who cared nothing for me cause me to eschew marriage completely."

"I beg your pardon, Jerome; I didn't even see you. I was very intentionally not looking at anyone, I was so scared to receive the 'cut direct' from one of my former friends. You don't know how hard it was for me to even make an appearance at the theatre that night."

"I can understand, now. But at the time it seemed to confirm that you'd never cared for me as I had for you, and I was determined not to wear the willow for you a moment longer. However, if you seemed too young when there was just four years separating us, imagine how childish the ladies making their come-out at seventeen seem to me now that I'm two-and-thirty. I chose Mrs. Boyle's name from that ridiculous directory precisely because she was unknown to London society, was no debutante, and did not live in town. And then, of course, after I'd called on her, I saw you at the theatre again, and you finally acknowledged me; you smiled at me. I cannot tell you how beautiful a sight that was, your smile. I had been missing it these eleven years. At first I was just relieved to have you again as my friend, but I also thought, now that there was no betrothal between us, I could show you that you were the bride I would choose of my own free will, if I were allowed to make that choice."

Regina couldn't believe what she was hearing. It was what she'd wanted Jerome to say to her since she was fifteen, although she would never have admitted it to him at the time. She remembered her father leaving them in the room alone together so that Jerome could formally propose, and when she'd accepted him, all he'd done was shake hands with her. Then, when he made no romantic overtures over the next two years, she was convinced he had no feelings for her at all, and that by eloping with another man she would be freeing him from an unwanted marriage. She'd had no idea he was being noble and waiting for her to grow up, or that he'd been as pleased with the match as she had been.

"You're not fifteen any longer, Regina," Jerome said huskily, tilting her chin up.

"How kind of you to remind me," she said, and he laughed, before growing serious again.

"May I kiss you now?" he asked her, sounding almost shy.

Regina felt shy herself, and merely nodded in response. His kiss was tentative at first, as if she were still the young girl he'd been betrothed to and not the woman of eight-and-twenty she was today. But after that first light kiss, he pulled back and smiled at her, a smile that was so warm and joyful that it felt like a caress in itself. Then he took her much more securely into his arms and kissed her in earnest.

When Diana finally returned to the drawing room, the couple were seated on the sofa together, holding hands, though Lord Jerome politely rose as Diana entered the room. Diana took one look at their glowing faces and rushed over to Regina's side.

"Will you congratulate me, Diana?" Regina asked. "Jerome and I are engaged. Again," she said, with an irrepressible grin.

"I will not congratulate *you* Regina, but Lord Jerome." Diana turned to Jerome. "You are a very fortunate man, sir, and I offer my sincere congratulations."

"You are right, Mrs. Boyle. I do not deserve my good fortune," he said, with an adoring look at his fiancée.

"When will you marry? Have you decided?" Diana asked, and then realized that she would be affected by their answer as well. If they were to marry soon, she would need to return to Whitley House. She was truly happy and excited for her friend, but the thought of going back to Whitley House with Lucius and Mildred both in residence was a daunting one.

"We see no need for another long engagement," Regina said, confirming Diana's fears, "but we have not set a definite date."

"Will you have the banns called or marry by special license?" Diana asked.

Regina looked inquiringly at Lord Jerome. "Whatever you wish, Regina," he said. "My preference would be to marry in the next fortnight by special license. I see no need to wait, but I am not sure how long it will take you to prepare and I do not want to rush you."

"I've been prepared to marry you since I was fifteen, so it shouldn't take long at all. And special licenses are so fashionable, and you know I always like to be in fashion," she said, with a roll of her eyes indicating that she was joking about her fall from grace.

"I do think marrying Lord Jerome should restore your reputation," Diana said. "Society can hardly expel you for breaking your engagement and eloping with another man when you're married to the man you ostensibly wronged. That is, if you even want anything more to do with London society."

"At this moment I'm so happy I can forgive everyone," Regina said, with a sweep of her arm, "even Lady Jersey."

"Let's not invite her to the wedding, however," Lord Jerome said, not inclined to be as forgiving as his bride, and looking much more familiar to Diana with his usual satirical expression. She had hardly recognized this new, humbler Lord Jerome, but was thrilled that he had been so transformed by love for her friend. She soon made an excuse to leave the couple alone together again and was in the back parlor doing some needlework when Regina went looking for her a little while later.

"There you are. You didn't have to run away, you know," Regina told her.

"I figured you and Lord Jerome had wedding plans to

discuss," Diana said. "And I should probably start making my own plans to return to Whitley House."

"Don't be silly, Diana! You are my guest, whether I am married or not. Jerome will feel similarly, I'm sure."

"Regina, you're the one being silly. I couldn't intrude upon a pair of newlyweds."

Regina was stymied for a moment. "Well, perhaps you could go home to Whitley House the week after the wedding, but then you're welcome to return here."

"I don't know, Regina. I cannot live with you permanently, you know. I do have to go back to my own home sooner or later."

Regina sighed. "I suppose you do. It's such a shame. It's been lovely having you here."

"I've enjoyed it, too. I can't remember the last time I've been so happy," Diana said, and the two women smiled at each other.

"Speaking of your home, Jerome told me that he will be back at noon with Mr. Dean, who is hiring a chaise for the trip."

"You still mean to go to Whitley House?" Diana asked. "I completely understand if you'd rather spend time alone with Lord Jerome. It's not every day you become engaged."

"And it seems a wonderful way to celebrate the engagement, on an excursion with our closest friends," Regina assured her.

14

M R. DEAN AND Lord Jerome arrived promptly at noon, and the foursome started off on the hour-long journey to Whitley House. Lord Jerome and Regina were in a state of dazed euphoria, still unable to believe that they'd found their way back to each other after so many years. Diana felt a little uncomfortable observing their loving glances and furtive touches, and finally forced herself to look out the window so that she did not seem like a Peeping Tom. She was too embarrassed to look at Mr. Dean and so had no idea how he was coping with their lovestruck companions.

Diana still found herself ambivalent about this trip and could not understand why she had such a dread of visiting her own home. She knew that she would have to face up to this ridiculous fear and overcome it, especially now that Regina was soon to be married. Diana had lived with *two* disagreeable, curmudgeonly persons for five years before Mr. Boyle's death; surely she could live with only Mildred again. (Once Mr. Dean succeeded in getting rid of Lucius, that is, and she believed that he would.) But she had felt so free these last two months with Regina. To have a sympathetic friend, one who did not look at you with disapproval and disdain but with affection and respect, had been so very refreshing. And, if she were honest with herself, it wasn't just Regina whom she would miss.

She darted a glance at Mr. Dean, who sat beside her on the bench, and found he was staring at her. And the look in his eyes stole the breath from her body. There was the same passionate adoration that she'd seen in Lord Jerome's eyes when he looked at Regina, but when it was directed at her by Mr. Dean, it was infinitely more affecting. And, of course, Diana found Mr. Dean, or *Maxwell,* as she'd started calling him in her thoughts, ten times more attractive than Lord Jerome. Even now, when he only touched her with his gaze, she felt herself trembling, especially when she recalled how it had felt when he'd touched her with more than a look.

Could it be that she, who had vehemently proclaimed that she would never marry, was considering marrying again? And to a self-proclaimed fortune hunter? Was she a complete idiot? As she sat there, staring helplessly back into Maxwell's eyes, which appeared a dark gray in the carriage's dim interior, she certainly felt like one.

She was distracted when the carriage turned onto the

drive at Whitley House, and she tore her gaze away from Mr. Dean.

"We have arrived," Diana said, and Regina stopped looking adoringly at Lord Jerome to look out at her surroundings.

Diana felt the pride of ownership as they pulled up in front of the simple but elegant villa, built a century ago for a rich duke's mistress on eighty acres of parkland. George Boyle, the father of Mildred and Percival and a wealthy barrister, bought it from the woman's son in 1761. Percival, Diana's future husband, was just three years old at the time and Mildred hadn't yet been born. The house wasn't overwhelmingly grand, but its white stucco façade gleamed in the afternoon sun, and Diana preferred its compact elegance to an oversized, elaborate structure.

"It's beautiful, Diana," Regina said, as the carriage drew to a stop on the circular drive.

They stepped down from the carriage and Godfrey came out to meet them, directing the coachman to the stables before turning to Diana. She was shocked to find that she was happy to see the far-from-subservient "servant." Perhaps it was merely that she had grown so accustomed to seeing him every day, for so many years, that she just *thought* that she missed him. Whatever the case, she smiled at him and said, "I have brought guests, Godfrey, but we are only staying a few hours. Is Mildred at home?"

"Unfortunately not, ma'am. I believe she went to town to call upon you. With her . . . nephew, Mr. Lucius Boyle."

(Maxwell, who was at Diana's side, did not miss the slight hesitation before the butler said the word "nephew.")

"It is unfortunate that you did not make us aware you were coming," Godfrey continued. "You and Miss Boyle must have crossed each other en route."

Diana, though she didn't contradict him, thought it was actually extremely fortunate she had not informed them she was coming. In fact, she couldn't believe her good fortune, and turned happily to Regina and Jerome, who were behind her and Mr. Dean. "Mr. and Miss Boyle apparently went to town to call upon us, Regina."

"How unfortunate to have missed them," Regina said, with a look of feigned disappointment.

"Indeed," Diana agreed, but restrained herself from laughing at Regina as she wanted to, because of Godfrey's presence. Instead, she led her guests into the house and to the drawing room, requesting that Godfrey bring refreshments, and pointing out features of the house along the way.

Once they were seated in the drawing room Mr. Dean asked Diana, "Could I see the book you wanted to show me?"

"Certainly," Diana said, standing and leading him to a bookshelf, from which she pulled out a heavy Bible.

"You wanted to show him a Bible, Diana? Are you going to give him a sermon, too?" Regina asked, and Diana made a face at her friend.

"He was curious about the Boyle family," Diana explained, but realizing Mr. Dean wanted to keep the reason for his involvement in her affairs private, said no more on the subject. Thankfully, the mention of sermons reminded Regina and Jerome that they needed to ask a member of the clergy to officiate at their wedding, and they began a low-voiced discussion about whom to ask, leaving Diana and Maxwell to peruse the Boyle family history in relative privacy.

Diana opened the Bible to the page where one of the Boyle forebears had begun writing a list of births and marriages. The first entry was dated 1730 and recorded the birth of George Boyle, Mildred's father. This was followed by George's marriage to Lucille in 1756, and then the birth of Percival in 1758.

"This is your late husband," Maxwell confirmed, pointing to that entry.

"Yes. Percival Boyle, born 1758. Then Mildred is the next entry, born in 1764."

"It appears their mother also died that year," Mr. Dean said, pointing to the entry that showed the death of Lucille Boyle in 1764, followed by the death of George Boyle in 1782. The next entry was Diana's marriage to Percival in July 1810, and then the death of Percival Boyle in December 1815. Diana figured it must have been Mildred who had taken over the recording of family history as a young woman, because the handwriting changed with the entry of George Boyle's death, and seemed to be the same hand that recorded both Percival Boyle's marriage to her and his death.

Diana and Mr. Dean looked through the brief entries again and Diana ran her finger over the list, stopping where a sibling should have been. There was no brother, the supposed father of Lucius Boyle. There were just two births listed after their father George's marriage: Mildred and Percival. There was not even any indication that George remarried after his wife Lucille's death and sired any other children. Diana and Maxwell exchanged looks; hers one of surprise, and his one of satisfaction, as he was pleased his theory had been proven correct.

"You realize what this means, don't you?" he asked in a low tone, and Diana nodded.

"I never realized family history could be so fascinating," Regina called out to them from across the room, just as a footman entered the room with a tray, followed by Godfrey. "Ah, here are the refreshments."

Diana closed the Bible and put it away, and she and Maxwell rejoined the other couple. Maxwell entertained them over tea by telling them the sad story of Robert Barker, who was the official printer to the king and produced many of the Bibles in England in the seventeenth century, including the one in Whitley House's drawing room. But in 1631 he made a costly mistake.

"In the book of Exodus, in the chapter that lists the Ten Commandments, he omitted a very important word," Mr. Dean said, and then paused to take a bite of scone.

"Was it the word 'neighbor's'?" Lord Jerome suggested, after mentally reviewing the account while Mr. Dean chewed his pastry. "As in: 'Thou shalt not covet thy *neighbor's* wife.'"

Regina giggled. "That would be a shame if it were a sin to covet thy own wife. I'm very impressed at your Bible knowledge, Jerome. I'm fairly certain I couldn't recite the Ten Commandments. Is there anything you don't know?" she asked him, with a fond look.

"He doesn't know the word that was omitted in Robert Barker's 1631 edition of the Bible," Mr. Dean retorted, with a challenging look at his friend. "It was even worse than *coveting* your neighbor's wife. It was in the verse that says 'Thou shalt not commit adultery' and they left out the word 'not.' The verse read: 'Thou *shalt* commit adultery.'"

"Oh, dear," said Diana, appalled. "That's truly terrible."

"It is, indeed," said Regina, and looked as if she didn't know whether to be horrified or amused.

"Did they chop off his head?" Jerome asked, almost sympathetically.

"He and his co-publisher had their printer's licenses revoked, were fined three hundred pounds, and were imprisoned," Maxwell said.

"That's a pretty egregious error, but you can't help feeling sorry for the poor chap," Jerome said. "There are *a lot* of words in the Bible."

"And it was a very *short* word," Regina said, which, for some reason, seemed extremely funny to Diana, who broke into giggles.

Shortly afterward, their refreshments finished, Diana

took them on a tour of the house, pointing out two of her favorite features: the hand-painted chinoiserie wallpaper in the dining room and the green damask on the walls of an upstairs bedchamber.

"I recently replaced the damask, as it had faded quite horribly in the ninety years since the house was built," Diana explained, "though the Chinese wallpaper is original."

"Did you sew this as well?" Regina asked, pointing to an elaborate scene in needlework on the cushion of a chair.

"I did," Diana said, smiling. "It's a view of the grotto from the southwest side of the house, overlooking the river."

"It's beautiful," Mr. Dean said, looking at it more carefully. "You are very talented."

"She is," Regina agreed. "She creates the most incredible embroidery. Every day when our callers leave, she pulls out a piece of cloth and diligently works away at it."

"I was so excited when Regina took me to see Mary Linwood's exhibition in Leicester Square. She is a true artist," Diana said. "Have you gentlemen seen it? She has re-created many famous paintings using needle and thread, with the thread actually resembling brushwork. She even uses silk thread to create highlights."

"I saw it a few years ago," Maxwell said. "I found it very impressive. Her work looks so much like the original paintings, but has its own unique beauty."

Lord Jerome admitted he had not been to the famous needlewoman's exhibition. "I will take you after we are married, Jerome," Regina told him, "since this is one subject where my knowledge surpasses yours."

"I am sure there are many such subjects, my love," Jerome replied, kissing her hand. "And you'll find me a willing pupil."

Diana thought only Lord Jerome could make the most innocent of sentences sound like an improper suggestion, and rolling her eyes and shaking her head, she led her guests back downstairs to begin a tour of the exterior of the house.

AFTER DIANA GAVE them an overview of the grounds, pointing out the grotto and some of the other landmarks, the two couples separated. Regina and Jerome headed for the Sweet Walk, an aptly named path that had been planted with fragrant flowering trees and shrubbery, and Diana and Maxwell walked in the opposite direction, eventually arriving at an unoccupied cottage.

"We call it 'River House.' Not a very original name, I know, but it's even closer to the river than Whitley House. It was originally built as a greenhouse, I believe, and later used as an aviary before it was converted into a dwelling," Diana explained. The house was unlocked, and they let themselves in and stood talking in the front parlor, where the few pieces of furniture remaining were draped with holland covers. "When I first came to live at Whitley

House, there was a retired military officer renting it, but he left shortly before Mr. Boyle's death, and I haven't decided yet what to do with it. I suppose I'll eventually let it to someone again."

River House was smaller than the main house, though still a comfortable size, with two floors and four bedchambers. It was also very bright and light-filled, especially at the current moment, with the afternoon sunshine streaming in the front windows.

"It's very pleasant. Miss Boyle did not want to remove here after her brother's death?" Maxwell asked.

"Why, I don't think either of us even considered such a thing." Diana looked as if she had just experienced an epiphany. "What a marvelous idea!" she said, with a huge smile. But after a moment her face fell. "Though I doubt she'd agree to it."

"You have to do something about her, you know," Maxwell said. "You can't just come back to Whitley House and live with her as though nothing has happened. She must be aware that Lucius Boyle is not who he claims to be, which means she is trying to trick you into marrying him under false pretenses."

"Yes, I know. That's why I encouraged Regina and Lord Jerome to walk apart from us. I wanted your advice about what I should do. I'm such a coward that my initial reaction was to leave immediately and return to town without confronting her. But now I think we must wait until she returns, and I must speak to her privately. What I still do not understand is who Lucius Boyle really is and where she could have found him."

"Perhaps he's an actor she hired," Maxwell suggested.

"I can't imagine Mildred hiring an actor," Diana instinctively demurred, before sighing in resignation. "But then again, I can't imagine Mildred doing any of this. Although we've never been close, I would have never thought she'd actively conspire against me." The realization greatly depressed Diana, and suddenly overcome with fatigue, she pushed aside the covering on the sofa and sat down. She gestured to Maxwell that he could sit as well, but he merely propped himself against the opposite wall.

"Did her brother not leave her any of his fortune? I beg your pardon if the question sounds overly intrusive, but I am trying to understand what her motivation might be," Maxwell said.

"She was left a small sum; I believe her income works out to about a hundred pounds a year."

"And he left you both houses and everything else?" Maxwell asked, though it made him uncomfortable to do so. It could only remind Diana that he was already largely aware of the extent of her fortune, as he'd listed it in his directory. But Diana did not seem conscious of his discomfort, she was so distracted by Mildred's mysterious behavior.

"Yes," Diana said, "he left her only two thousand

pounds, from which she derives her income. I had never considered it before, but that was quite paltry."

"It does seem so, as it made her practically dependent upon you. He could have given her enough to set up her own establishment, or even left her this house in addition to the two thousand," Maxwell said.

"Poor Mildred. I feel foolish when we talk about it now, but I had never before thought about how that must sting. No wonder she is always sniping at me. She spent her entire life at Whitley House, and had to see it given to someone else."

"It still doesn't excuse her behavior, however," Maxwell reminded Diana.

"Not entirely, no. But it does help me to feel more sympathetic toward her."

Maxwell smiled at her. "I don't think you need any help to feel sympathy. You're the most kindhearted person I know."

"That's because you did not know my mother. She used to tell me that we are all the heroes of our own story, and we should stop and consider how the villain of the story might tell it."

"Your mother sounds like a wise woman. And while Mildred and Lucius do seem to be involved in a villainous scheme, it would be helpful to try to understand what may have led them to take this step. Perhaps your butler might also have some insight."

"Godfrey?" Diana asked, and then was silent for a

moment as she considered it. "You could very well be right. He's been at Whitley House for decades. We could have probably just asked him outright if Mildred and my late husband had ever had a brother; I'm sure he would know. And Lucius Boyle, or whoever he is, has been staying here for a few weeks now. Godfrey may have observed, or overheard, something."

Diana rose from the sofa with a sigh and turned to replace the cover. Before she could do so Maxwell rushed over to help her.

"Thank you. I suppose I should interview Godfrey before Mildred and the so-called Lucius Boyle return. I hate to encourage Godfrey, yet again, in his prying tendencies, though they have been of great benefit to me. He is the one who discovered the existence of your directory, and that you were the author," Diana told Maxwell.

"He sounds like he's wasting his talents as a butler," Maxwell said. "He should work for Bow Street."

"I wish he would. He doesn't make the most comfortable of butlers," Diana said, with a grimace.

They exited the house and stood for a moment in the front garden, looking out at the river. "It looks so peaceful, yet you don't seem to have found much peace here," Maxwell commented.

"I am at peace when I'm outside, like this, walking by the river or working in the garden. And I am fond of the house, but it has been a little like a golden cage," Diana said, as they began walking down the path that would eventually take them back to Whitley House. "I didn't realize how unhappy I was until I went to stay with Regina. I'm very glad for her and Jerome, of course, but I selfishly wish I never had to return here."

"I wish there was something I could do to ensure your happiness," said Maxwell, feeling frustrated by the futility of the words even as they left his mouth. "I know that the expression 'Your obedient servant' has become a commonplace one, with no deeper intent than to express a polite platitude. But I can think of no greater honor than to be of service to you. And I beg you always to think of me, sincerely and truly, as your obedient servant."

He had stopped walking and turned to face her, and she stopped walking as well, wondering, as her heart began to beat faster in anticipation, what he was about to do. She was surprised when he knelt down on one knee on the path before her, and bowed his head as if he were a knight paying homage to a queen. He then raised his head and, still kneeling, took her hand and brought it briefly to his lips.

Diana could think of nothing to say; it felt as if there was a solemn significance to this simple gesture, but he did not make her an offer of marriage as she half expected him to. He just stared up at her as if she were the goddess she'd been named for. She supposed if they were living in medieval times and he had sworn fealty to her, she would now be expected to tap him on each shoulder with a sword. She had no sword, of course, so she reached out and touched him on one shoulder and then the other, but instead of striking him she pressed very gently, brushing his shoulder lightly with her palm. This must have been the correct thing to do because he smiled at her when she had finished, a smile so brilliant that it caused her very toes to curl.

He then got up, brushed lightly at his breeches, and they began walking again. And Diana wished she had the courage to tell him that if it was his goal to ensure her happiness, he'd succeeded, because his very presence filled her with joy.

15

On the way back to the house, Maxwell offered to speak to Godfrey on Diana's behalf. "You're already anxious about having to speak to Miss Boyle, and I'd like to spare you at least one awkward interview," he said. "I'd willingly speak to Miss Boyle for you, as well, if I thought it would be helpful, but I am a stranger to her, and she'd be much less likely to confide in me."

"How kind of you to offer, but you're right, it's my responsibility to talk to Mildred. However, I will gladly allow you to speak to Godfrey. I suspect he dislikes women, or at least dislikes taking orders from one, so you would probably get much further with him than I would."

When they arrived at the house, Godfrey met them at the door, and Diana told him that she was going up to her room to refresh herself but that he should see to

Mr. Dean's comfort. Left in the hall together, Godfrey asked Mr. Dean how he could serve him.

"You could answer a few questions for me," Maxwell said, "about the man who is claiming to be Lucius Boyle."

"*Claiming* to be?" Godfrey asked, and Maxwell, studying Godfrey's expression, felt that he was not being untruthful. While Godfrey had appeared to hint earlier that Lucius was not Mildred's nephew, he was not now denying that was the man's name. This added an entirely new dimension to the affair, and Maxwell quickly thought of what that could mean in the face of the information he did possess.

"Come, Godfrey, I'm aware that he is *not* Miss Boyle's nephew." Godfrey did not contradict this statement, and Maxwell, who had arrived at what he felt was a logical conclusion, asked: "Is he the natural son of one of the Boyle men, either Percival or his father?"

Godfrey, whose expression rarely changed, couldn't prevent a slight look of surprise at this question, which he conveyed by blinking a few times in rapid succession. However, he then disappointed Maxwell by answering: "Not to my knowledge, sir, but it's not my place to say."

Maxwell wondered if he would get further by offering the man money for what he undoubtedly knew, because Max had no doubt he knew exactly who Lucius Boyle was. However, that could just as easily prove offensive and Godfrey, who was not being exactly forthcoming, could clam up altogether. So Max smiled at him, as if he just wanted to have a cordial chat. "How long have you been here at Whitley House, Godfrey?"

"I started nigh on four-and-thirty years ago, in 1783."

"Quite soon after George Boyle's death."

Godfrey just nodded, but looked a little suspicious, as if curious where Maxwell had obtained such exact information of the Boyle family.

"And it was just Mr. Boyle and his sister, Mildred, living here all that time? There were no other siblings?" Maxwell asked.

"There was just Mr. Boyle and his sister," Godfrey said. This confirmed what Maxwell and Diana had already discovered: there was no brother, at least no legitimate one.

"It's impressive that you have been in service with them for so many years; you've been loyal to the family for decades. However, Miss Boyle doesn't own Whitley House, *Mrs.* Boyle does. Wouldn't you like to display your loyalty to her?" Maxwell asked Godfrey, in what he felt was a very reasonable manner.

Godfrey's controlled demeanor finally cracked a little, and some of his true feelings emerged. "I am loyal to them that are loyal to me. Thirty-three years I served that man; knew more about him and his sister than they knew about each other, and kept it to myself, thinking he'd reward me in the end. But no, not Percival Boyle. He respected no one, man or maid. When they read the will, he commended me for my faithful service and left me a broken old watch. He gave all the money, anything of value to *her,* who hated the very sight of him," Godfrey said, dropping his proper mien and letting his bitterness show in his tone and on his face. But he quickly had himself back under control when he heard a carriage on the front drive.

"Tell Mrs. Boyle that in proof of my loyalty to her, I would recommend she ask Miss Boyle about the circumstances surrounding Lucius Boyle's birth, as Miss Boyle was present on that occasion." Godfrey said this with a significant look that made it clear Mildred was not just a bystander. "That is all I will say on the matter, especially as I hear a carriage arriving. Most likely Miss Boyle and Mr. Lucius Boyle have returned," he said, and he left Maxwell to go to the door.

Maxwell, shocked by what he had just been told and even more shocked by what he had then surmised, did not want to be caught standing in the hallway by Mildred and Lucius when they entered the house. He also wanted to give Diana some warning before she spoke to Mildred. He realized it was extremely inappropriate for a gentleman to enter a lady's chamber, but he could think of no other way to speak to her before Mildred did. He went up to the second floor and began knocking on doors and was quite relieved when Diana finally appeared at one.

"What is it, what happened?" she asked him, motioning for him to enter her room and quickly closing the door once he did so.

"I beg your pardon, Mrs. Boyle—" Maxwell began, but Diana interrupted him.

"Mr. Dean, this is becoming a little ridiculous. I think we've reached the stage in our relationship, especially now that you're standing here in my bedchamber, where you can call me Diana." She was blushing as she said this, and smiling shyly, but she managed to raise her eyes to meet his.

"Diana," he said softly, returning her smile. And then he repeated her name again, in a firmer tone: "Diana, I would much rather talk about what stage you think we've reached in our relationship, and I would also like to hear you address me as Maxwell, or Max, if you prefer. But unfortunately, Mildred and Lucius Boyle have arrived and we must instead discuss them. Which is the last thing I'd like to do, having just been invited into a beautiful woman's bedchamber."

They continued to smile silently at each other for a moment more before he reluctantly changed the subject to the most awkward and unromantic one he could ever imagine having to discuss with her. "From what I just learned from Godfrey, I think that Lucius might be *Mildred's* son."

"What? That's impossible. Mildred never married," Diana said, speaking the last sentence slowly and emphatically, as if he might be deficient in understanding.

"I am aware of that. However, it is possible to bear children even if one is not married," he told her, feeling as if he was explaining to a six-year-old who staunchly believed in them that there were no such things as fairies.

"It's not possible; you must have misunderstood. Mildred would never— Why, the very notion is preposterous!"

Maxwell could understand why she had a difficult time accepting such a thing; Mildred Boyle was not the type of woman you'd suspect of ever having been a participant in any sort of scandalous behavior. But she hadn't always been a fifty-three-year-old spinster.

"I know it seems hard to believe, but that's the only explanation that makes sense. It's true that I might have misunderstood, or that Godfrey purposely led me to the wrong conclusion. But I didn't want you to speak to Mildred without first knowing that she might be Lucius's mother." Diana still looked shocked and overwhelmed, so Maxwell smiled at her and briefly clasped her hand. "This is your opportunity to display the forgiving attitude your mother taught you, as well as to suspend judgment until you learn the entire story."

"You are right. If it is true—" She stopped and sighed. "Poor Mildred."

At just that moment they heard the voice of "poor Mildred" from outside the door, accompanied by a loud knock. "Diana! Godfrey tells me you're here."

Diana and Maxwell looked at each other, their eyes big. "This is terrible," Diana said. "She'll be sure to think—" And then she realized the foolishness of worrying what Mildred might think about her, and she and Maxwell smiled at each other.

"Even if she did claim that you're compromised when

she finds me here, the last thing she'd want is for you to marry *me*," Maxwell said, and Diana felt a pang of disappointment that Mildred *wouldn't* insist they marry.

"Diana! Are you talking to someone?" Mildred asked, rattling the doorknob. Diana had not locked it, and she and Mr. Dean turned to face the door at the exact same moment Mildred opened it.

Mildred was so surprised by the sight of Mr. Dean in Diana's bedchamber that she was unable to speak for what might have been the first time in her life. She just stood there and gasped, her plump cheeks and panting mouth making her look like a fish that had just been dragged to shore and was taking its last desperate breaths.

"Come in, Mildred. Mr. Dean had just come up to tell me you had arrived," Diana calmly told her, and then turned to Mr. Dean and said, "I would like to speak to my sister-in-law in private, so perhaps you could wait for us in the drawing room. And if Lord Jerome and Lady Regina return from their walk, could you please tell them I'll be down as soon as I've finished my conversation with Miss Boyle?"

Mr. Dean bowed to the two women and left the room, and Diana gestured for Mildred to sit on a chair by the window. Mildred did so, but she had finally regained her voice and told Diana how shocked she had been to find Mr. Dean in her room. "I know you're a widow and thus permitted a little more license than an unmarried woman, but you should be careful of your reputation, nonetheless."

"Thank you for the warning, Mildred, but I am not in the habit of inviting gentlemen into my bedchamber," Diana said.

Mildred opened her mouth to reply, and then closed it and her eyes as well. Diana watched her, wondering what this odd behavior signified. She hoped Mildred was not having a stroke. But then Mildred opened her eyes, swallowed visibly, and said, "I beg your pardon, Diana. I know you are a virtuous woman and that your relationship with Mr. Dean is—none of my affair."

Diana was so taken aback by this uncharacteristic response that she did not know how to reply. Though she agreed with Mildred that she should mind her own business, she could hardly say so. But it appeared Mildred did not expect a reply, because after a moment she began speaking again. "I had actually gone to town today to confess to you that I had encouraged Lucius to call on you with the goal of seeing the two of you make a match. I am exceedingly fond of Lucius, he is . . . almost like a son to me, and in my anxiety to see him settled, I ignored *your* wishes entirely. I realize your match with my brother was not by your choice, and it was . . ." She paused to clear her throat. ". . . wrong of me to try to coerce you into another such marriage. Lucius will no longer attempt to court you. Indeed, it was his suggestion that I apologize to you so that you could feel free to return to Whitley House without fearing he would pester you with unwanted attentions."

She had been telling Diana all of this while staring

down at her hands, which she held clasped together tightly
in her lap, but she finally looked up and met Diana's gaze,
and said a little defiantly: "Although Lucius is an admira-
ble young man and I believe he would have made you a
fine husband."

"I am sure he is, Mildred," Diana said gently. "But are
you being entirely truthful when you say that he is 'almost' like a son to you?"

Mildred turned so white Diana thought she might
faint, and she rushed to Mildred's side, grabbing one of her
hands and chafing it. "I am very sorry; it was unkind of
me to mention it so abruptly."

Mildred stared at Diana a moment more, before she
licked her lips and took a deep breath. "Who told you?
Was it Godfrey?"

"Not in so many words. But he did confirm that Lucius
was not your nephew and suggested I speak to you."

"Who else knows? Did you tell Lady Regina and Lord
Jerome? Lady Gordon? Does all of London know of my
shame?" Mildred asked, and Diana's soft heart was touched
when she saw a tear run down Mildred's very pale cheek.

"Only Mr. Dean knows, and it's because he suspected
Lucius was not who he claimed to be and wanted to help
me. But neither he, nor I, will tell anyone. The only thing
I care about is why you would play such a trick on me,"
Diana said, and though she was trying her best to guard
her tongue, she couldn't help but let some of her disappointment become evident in her tone.

"I just wanted to provide for Lucius. As you discovered, I'm his mother, and I've never been able to give him *anything*," Mildred said, before she began sobbing so violently that Diana was frightened for her health. She had never touched Mildred in her life until just a few moments ago when she had grabbed her hand, but now she found herself hugging the older woman and patting her back to try to calm her.

Mildred's sobs eventually quieted, although she was still shivering, and Diana told her she would go get a glass of water. "No, Diana," Mildred said, her teeth chattering. "I want to explain . . . I don't want you to think even worse of me than you must already."

"I don't think badly of you, Mildred," Diana protested, though that was not entirely true. However, she was disappointed in Mildred for lying to her and trying to trick her into marriage, not for any mistakes she may have made in the past.

"How could you not?" Mildred said, and Diana was glad to see that she had finally stopped shivering. "What a hypocrite you must think me, to lecture you so frequently about your behavior, when you know I've done far worse. But I could not tell you, could not tell anyone, that Lucius was really my son. He would be blamed for my sins and denied a place in society. That is why I could not reveal my secret; it was more for his sake than my own."

Diana handed Mildred a handkerchief and they sat in silence for some time. And then Mildred began to tell her story in a soft voice that Diana didn't recognize. She wondered if this was how Mildred had sounded as a young woman, before what she'd experienced had embittered her.

"I was an heiress at one time, too, you know," Mildred said, "though I was never as pretty as you. My father died before I could come out and then Percival was always so unsociable; I was as naïve and gullible as a child, although I was twenty-one when I met Lucius's father, John.

"It was my very first ball. I had somehow been invited to Horace Walpole's, probably because they knew I was an heiress. John was a guest there, and he seemed so suave and sophisticated, such a different creature from anyone I'd ever met in my poor sheltered life. Percival disliked him from the first and told me he was only after my money, which turned out to be true, but I wouldn't believe it. I loved John, and I believed him when he said he loved me.

"He convinced me to elope with him, telling me that Percival would never give us permission to marry. He knew I was of age, so he thought I was already in possession of my fortune. He didn't realize that my father had left it under Percival's control, and that I would only receive it if I married someone Percival approved of. I wasn't aware of it, either, as neither Percival nor my father ever spoke to me about money, and I assumed it already belonged to me. So both John and I were ignorant of the fact that I wasn't *really* in possession of a fortune, and under that misconception we made our way to Gretna Green. But it's a very long way to Scotland, and it took even longer thirty years ago, when the roads weren't what they are now. We had to stop at an inn on three nights, and although I insisted on separate rooms on the first night, the second night there was only one room available, and John told them we were husband and wife, and then told me we were as near to that as made no difference." Mildred started crying again, and Diana waited patiently for her to regain her composure, making little consoling noises until she did so. "So he ruined me, and I told myself that it didn't matter; because as he'd said, we'd be husband and wife in just a few days.

"However, Percival caught up with us the morning of the last leg of our journey, and explained to John that I was *not* in possession of my fortune, and that I would never receive it unless he approved the marriage. John told him that I was ruined, that no one else would marry me, and that it would only make sense for Percival to accept our marriage and release my fortune to him. At this point I realized John didn't love me, he had never loved me, but I figured I had made my bed"—Mildred made a wry grimace at her choice of words—"and I must now lie in it. I was still willing to marry him; indeed, I knew I had no choice. It never occurred to me that Percival would not agree to release my fortune. And without a fortune, John would no longer marry me."

"Oh, Mildred, that's terrible!"

"I was devastated, but Percival refused to change his mind, and would not listen to any of my pleas. We came back to Whitley House and I knew that, now that I had lost my reputation, I would spend the rest of my life here, with a brother whom I hated. And, as despicable as John had proved himself to be, I still mourned the loss of the love I'd had for him. But I soon found my life was destined to become even harder, because as you've no doubt realized, I later found out I was pregnant. I begged Percival to give me my fortune and let me marry John after all, and he might have, as he hated the thought of me bearing a bastard child even more than I did, but in those few months we were apart, John had found himself a new heiress and had married her."

"No!" Diana said, shocked. "The man sounds like a complete scoundrel, Mildred. I am sorry that Percival wouldn't give you your fortune so you could have married, but perhaps you were better off without him."

"I don't think so, Diana. At least if he'd married me, I would have been able to . . . keep my child," she said, the last words coming out as a whisper as she fought to maintain her fragile composure. "Percival sent me away when it was no longer possible to hide my pregnancy, and it was at some remote hired cottage that I had the baby. The morning after Lucius was born, Percival arrived with a nursemaid and took Lucius away from me. They pulled him from my arms, and it made no difference that he screamed and cried and so did I. Percival wouldn't even tell me where he'd had him taken, even though I asked him repeatedly over the years. And Godfrey, whom I suspected

Percival told and who was a footman at the time, was promoted to butler. I think it pleased Percival to have someone here at Whitley House who knew my humiliating secret.

"It wasn't until after Percival died that it suddenly occurred to me that I might be able to discover where Lucius had been sent. I went to our man of affairs, who was no longer bound to keep it secret, and he told me where payments had been sent for the first eighteen years of Lucius's life. He was raised in a vicarage, by a vicar who already had a large family, and Percival gave them fifty pounds a year to house him. Fifty pounds a year! Less than he spent on wine! And then when Lucius was eighteen and the allowance ended, his foster family put him out with the clothes on his back. He stayed in sporadic contact with them, however, and they told me he had gone to London and was working as a bank clerk.

"And then, after I finally found Lucius, it occurred to me that, even though Percival was already rotting in his grave, I could still have my revenge on him. I could put Lucius in Percival's place. I could give *him* Percival's wife, Percival's house, and all the money Lucius and I were entitled to that Percival never gave us and gave to you instead. If you want the truth, Diana, I think that's the reason why my brother married you. He knew that if he didn't have some other heir then he would have to leave Whitley House to me, and he couldn't bear to do so.

"So that is why I tried to trick you into marrying

Lucius. I said he was Percival's nephew because he was, and I did want to stick to the truth as closely as possible. But of course he was not *my* nephew, and he was definitely not Percival's favorite relation," Mildred said, with an ironic smile. "Lucius wasn't enthusiastic about the scheme, but went along with it to appease me. However, while he was willing to meet you and even marry you if he thought you favored his suit, he had come to realize you did not, and we had gone to visit you today because, as I told you earlier, we were going to apologize and confess. Oh, not about Lucius being my son—I had still hoped to keep his illegitimacy a secret—but that I had promoted the match for my own purposes and would cease doing so."

Mildred looked completely wrung out by the end of her confession, her face mottled and blotchy, her eyes and nose red. Diana thought it so strange that she'd lived in the same house with Mildred for years and knew nothing of the tragedy that had marked her life; that she'd kept such a distressing secret completely hidden.

"Thank you for telling me all of this, Mildred. I am so sorry for all that you've suffered," Diana said, and Mildred looked up, an expression of surprise on her ravaged face. She had been sitting with her shoulders slumped and eyes downcast, awaiting some sort of judgment and sentence from Diana, and this expression of sympathy was far from what she'd been expecting to hear.

"No, I am the one who is sorry," Mildred said. "By the time Percival married you, I had forgotten how to show kindness and only knew how to hurt and be hurt. I've treated you very ill, indeed. I hope that you can forgive me. If you find that you can, perhaps we could . . . begin again." Mildred's voice had almost petered out completely by the time she finished this speech, and Diana had to lean forward to hear her.

"I would like that very much," Diana said.

MILDRED WENT TO her own room, but stopped Diana as she was passing by on her way downstairs. "I assume you will ask Lucius to leave Whitley House," Mildred said, and her lower lip trembled a little. "Would it be possible for him to stay another few nights? He will have to look for another position and find lodging."

"Of course he can stay a few nights. In fact, please tell him not to search for lodging until you and I have had an opportunity to speak again. As long as he promises to leave off his pursuit of me, I have no objection to your son visiting you," Diana said. "And Lucius can continue to be known as your nephew, if that's what you both prefer. It is only Mr. Dean and I who are aware of the truth, and we will keep your secret." Mildred's grateful smile caused Diana to realize it had been her perpetual scowl that had obscured her features and caused her to look disagreeable. The smile transformed Mildred, and Diana could see her resemblance to Lucius, who, now that he would no longer be harassing her with his attentions, Diana could admit was a handsome man.

Diana was very relieved that she would soon be rid of her unwanted suitor, and she was also much more at peace with the prospect of returning to Whitley House now that she and Mildred had come to an understanding. She still felt a pang at the thought of leaving Regina and the other friends she'd made the past two months in London, but she would not be saying goodbye forever; she'd only be a short drive away.

She was partway down the stairs when she saw Maxwell standing in the doorway of the drawing room, looking anxiously up at her. It appeared that he'd been waiting there for some time so that he would be able to see her as soon as she came down after her conversation with Mildred. He looked a question at her, and she nodded and smiled, and his own expression changed from concern to relief. She felt warmed to the bone by the realization that her feelings mattered so much to him; that *she* mattered so much to him.

He stopped her to briefly ask, "Was what we assumed correct?"

"Yes, I'll explain it all to you later," Diana said and, entering the drawing room, she saw that Regina and Jerome had come back from their walk and were talking to Lucius.

"Is Miss Boyle coming down?" Lady Regina asked.

"Unfortunately not. She is indisposed. If you are ready, I believe we can head back to town," Diana said, and the others agreed that they were ready to depart. Diana went to ask Godfrey to call for the carriage and, before he left to do so, said to him, "Thank you, Godfrey, for your discretion."

"Of course, ma'am," Godfrey said, his face expressionless, as befitted a good butler.

DIANA TOLD THE others in the carriage ride back to town that Mildred had admitted she'd been encouraging Lucius to pursue her but had agreed to tell him to cease his attentions.

"I feel much happier about returning to Whitley House now," Diana said. "Indeed, Mildred and I seem to have reached an understanding." She looked at Maxwell as she said this, and he smiled approvingly at her.

"I am so glad, Diana," Regina said. "It was terrible that you felt so uncomfortable about returning to your own home. To be honest, I'll be happy to see less of Lucius Boyle myself."

The conversation then turned to Regina and Jerome's wedding plans. They had decided to marry in two weeks in the drawing room of Regina's townhouse, with only a few guests. "Just you and Mr. Dean, and Lady Gordon. We will write to invite my brother and his wife, and Jerome's brother as well, but we doubt they will come."

"My brother was in town earlier in the year and left just

a few weeks ago to return to his estate in Lincolnshire," Jerome explained.

"And now that you're feeling more comfortable about going to Whitley House, Jerome and I will probably take a wedding trip and visit our family. They will be very happy to hear that their plans for us have finally come to fruition," Regina said.

Diana realized that she and Maxwell would have no privacy to discuss what she'd *really* learned from Mildred, so when he dropped her and Regina back at their house and asked if he could take Diana on a drive two days later, she readily agreed. She and Regina had no engagements for the evening, and Diana was glad to have solitude to consider the situation with Mildred. She eventually thought of a way to mitigate the injustice that had been done, but she did not want to make a decision too quickly and later regret her impetuousness. However, as she said her prayers that night before going to bed, she felt more at peace with herself and her decision than she had since the dreadful day she'd become Mrs. Boyle.

16

THE NEXT MORNING, Diana called on Lady Gordon to tell her about Regina's engagement and ask if she would consent to co-host another ball at her home. "I would like this one to be in honor of Regina and Lord Jerome's engagement, if you are agreeable."

"Why, that is a splendid idea!" Lady Gordon said. "What a perfect way to re-establish Lady Regina's position in society!"

"Then you think people will come?" Diana asked.

"Certainly they will come. They will beg us for an invitation," Lady Gordon said, and it was the first time Diana had seen her look like the haughty aristocrat she undoubtedly was. However, that impression was dispelled an instant later when Monsieur de la Tour was announced, and Lady Gordon blushed a fiery red.

The three greeted one another, Diana expressing her

delight in seeing Monsieur again, as this was the first opportunity she'd had to do so since the Vauxhall excursion.

"Monsieur de la Tour is escorting me to Richmond," Lady Gordon said, "but we will be back this evening, and if you will call on me again tomorrow, Diana, we can begin planning the ball."

Diana wished them both a good day and returned to Regina's townhouse, where she told Regina what she and Lady Gordon were planning. "So now, in addition to a wedding dress, you should also think about what dress you will wear to your ball," Diana said. "We will hold it on the evening before your wedding, if that is agreeable to you and Lord Jerome."

"Oh, Diana, how exciting!" Regina said. "And how kind of you and Lady Gordon!"

"Not at all," Diana said, with a dismissive gesture. "It is the least I could do to repay you for your kindness to me. Although there is really no way I could ever do so."

The friends smiled at each other and then Regina said, "I know that it was wrong of Mr. Dean to publish that directory, but I cannot help but be glad that he did. Imagine if he hadn't, none of this would have happened. You and I would have never met; we would not have come to know Lady Gordon and the other Ladies of the Registry; Jerome and I wouldn't be getting married—"

"And I would not have reconciled with my sister-in-law," Diana added.

"So, since Mr. Dean is not the villain you originally

thought him, has he redeemed himself enough in your eyes for you to consider marrying him?"

"Mr. Dean hasn't *asked* me to marry him," Diana said, and though she attempted to sound as if it made no difference to her that he hadn't, she knew that her tone betrayed her.

"Oh, come now, Diana, it's perfectly obvious that he adores you. He probably feels that he cannot propose since he's infamous for being the creator of that document. How is he to prove to you that he isn't pursuing you for your fortune? Though, to be perfectly candid, a few of the other ladies would be happy to have him for a husband, and even attempted to divert his attention from you, with no success."

"That is rather traitorous of them," Diana said, with a frown.

"Not necessarily. You've made no secret of the fact that *you* didn't want him. And you've also made it clear that you weren't interested in marrying again. They may have felt they'd be doing you a favor."

Diana knew better than to believe that. Any lady who attempted to steal Maxwell's affections from her wasn't doing so as an unselfish act of benevolence. However, Regina was correct in saying that she had made it obvious she had no interest in marriage. She'd even told Maxwell so! How did she now go about signifying that she had changed her mind?

Because she had changed her mind, most definitely.

The thought of parting from Maxwell, even temporarily, was unbearable. And the thought of him marrying someone else, which he surely would eventually do if Diana did not marry him, was even more distressing to contemplate.

Her first marriage she now discounted completely. It should never have happened, and she would not use it as a gauge of her future happiness with someone else. She had often wondered why Mr. Boyle had married her; he was not the type to make a chivalrous or generous gesture, and she knew he had not been in love with her any more than she had been with him. But now that Mildred had told her story, Diana realized that spite might have led him to marry her; he was a very spiteful, petty man. It was a large part of the reason she'd been so unhappy in her marriage. As unattractive and unlikable as she'd found him, she had tried her best to do as her mother instructed and show him respect, but she'd found it impossible to *feel* any respect for him. However now, looking back, she was pleased that, as young as she was, she'd at least attempted to hide her disdain and dislike from him; it had been a constant struggle to swallow contemptuous words and reply to him and Mildred in a dignified manner. She knew she probably hadn't always been successful, and to some extent he must have guessed her true feelings, but Diana's conscience was clear. She would no longer hold herself to blame for the failure of that disastrous union and her feelings of relief at its ending, even if that ending had been caused by Mr. Boyle's death.

She still believed that to marry for money was the worst mistake a person could make and was resolved never to be a participant in that sort of marriage again. But, like Regina, she did not think Mr. Dean solely interested in her fortune; she had come to believe he was in love with her. There were dozens of other ladies listed in his directory who had no objection to marriage, yet he had not pursued any of them. If his intention was merely to marry a woman for her fortune, he'd certainly had many other opportunities to do so. But he had put himself at Diana's service. He had rid her of Lucius Boyle's attentions, as he'd promised he would, and had proclaimed himself her "obedient servant" purely for the honor of serving her, with no prospect of a reward.

She did not think it necessary to test his love for her; she believed it was sincere. But she knew the decision she'd come to in regard to Mildred's situation would test Maxwell's true feelings for her, whether she'd planned to do so or not. And when he passed this unlooked-for test, she'd have confirmation that her confidence in him was not misplaced.

MAXWELL ARRIVED THE following afternoon to take Diana driving in the park. He'd once again hired a vehicle as Diana still had not purchased a sporting carriage, and she knew now that she never would. There was no reason for her to do so if she was leaving London and Regina was getting married. But perhaps she could purchase a gig to use when she was back in Twickenham, now that Maxwell had taught her how to drive.

They went to Green Park, as Maxwell explained that it wasn't as popular as Hyde Park and he thought they would be able to speak there without interruption. Upon arriving he handed the reins over to the boy who had been perched up behind them. Diana didn't recognize him as the porter who had announced her arrival to Maxwell the first time they'd met, but she did notice that he had looked her over with more than a cursory interest.

"That's Jim," Maxwell told her as they walked away. "After you visited me in my rooms, he came to the unfounded conclusion that I am a veritable Don Juan and has been attempting to discover the secret of my success ever since."

Diana was reminded of what Regina had told her about other ladies pursuing Maxwell. "It can't have been merely my visit that led him to that conclusion," Diana said, a little suspiciously.

"Well, no," Maxwell said, and Diana could have sworn he reddened somewhat. "There were other lady visitors. But they did not come at my invitation, I assure you. In fact, I did my utmost to get rid of my last visitor before I inadvertently compromised her. I think she would have been happy at such an eventuality, though I'm as puzzled as Jim as to the reason."

Diana was not at all puzzled; she knew exactly why the

hussy had wanted Maxwell to compromise her. Diana
would love to be compromised by him herself, but didn't
know how to accomplish it. But that wasn't really true; she
wanted Max to propose because he wanted to, not because
he was forced to do so.

However, before they were able to talk about their relationship, she needed to first tell him that Mildred *was*
Lucius's mother, and also explain the rest of her tragic history, which she proceeded to do.

"How very sad. Poor Mildred," Maxwell said at the end
of it, and Diana felt such relief at his response that her
knees grew weak. The man she loved was no misogynist
like her first husband. "Percival Boyle's treatment of his
sister seems to be very typical of him," Maxwell continued. "Godfrey told me Boyle did not leave him adequate
compensation, either, even though he's been at Whitley
House for more than thirty years."

Diana, who had resolved to do something for Mildred
and Lucius, added Godfrey to her mental list of those who
deserved recompense.

"I am sorry you were married to such a man. I already
knew he didn't deserve you, but I had no idea how very
unworthy he was," Maxwell said solemnly.

"It was never a true marriage," Diana said. "He married me to spite his sister, and I married him for a roof over
my head. That's why I've decided"—she stopped walking
so that she could look Maxwell in the face as she said the
next words—"to give Whitley House to Mildred."

He had halted as well and was looking down at her, and his expression seemed to be one of surprise and concern, if she interpreted it correctly. "But you love that house," he said.

Diana shrugged. "I liked making it more beautiful than it was already. But it's just a house. And Mildred was born there; it's her legacy, not mine. It never should have been mine. I also intend to split my inheritance with her. Percival never gave her her dowry, you know. It was supposed to have been ten thousand pounds, and that was over thirty years ago."

He studied her face for a few moments in silence. Then he smiled. "Just when I thought it was impossible for me to . . . admire you more," he said, and Diana wondered if his slight hesitation was because he had wanted to say "love" or if that was just wishful thinking on her part.

"Do not admire me too much," Diana said. "I *am* keeping River House."

"That is the perfect solution," Maxwell said, looking greatly relieved. "Because you do deserve *something* after having had to live with that blighter. I'm very glad that you will have suitable accommodations to remove to. A less generous person would have given River House to Mildred and kept Whitley House for themselves. That was my initial suggestion, you remember."

"Mildred dislikes the sound of the river," Diana said, with a smile and shake of her head at Mildred's quirks. "And this seems to me to be a more equitable solution.

Not to mention that I'm happy to have a fresh start in a home that has no unpleasant memories attached to it."

They walked a few more minutes in silence, before Diana said, "I will miss all of my friends here in town, however. I know that it will be far less convenient, but I hope that you will continue to call on me at River House after Regina and Lord Jerome are married." She felt foolish asking a man to call on her, and hoped he wouldn't think her as forward as those other ladies who had thrown themselves at him, but since he'd barely blinked at the news that she was giving away a mansion and half of her fortune, she thought it was now very plain that he had not been coveting her possessions. He had passed a test without even being aware that he was being tested, and she hoped he could now admit that he loved her.

"As to that, I also have some news to share with you," Maxwell said. "I will no longer be living in London, either. I accepted a post yesterday with the East India Company and am going to Calcutta. I sail the week after Regina and Jerome's wedding."

Diana, who had envisioned a future where Maxwell married her and they lived happily ever after at River House, couldn't fully comprehend what he was saying. "But . . . why?" were the only two words she could manage to utter.

"Because of you," Maxwell said. "Our so-called noble society has a very odd view of such matters, and you made me realize that I'd subscribed to that view. They consider any type of trade or labor beneath them, and not the province of a gentleman, but they think it perfectly acceptable to marry a wealthy woman to acquire a fortune. You've helped me to appreciate that the opposite is true: marrying for material advantage is not the act of a *true* gentleman, whereas engaging in an honest profession is, in actuality, the noble course. And I do have an aptitude for documentation and figures, as my directory has proved. I thought I'd put that skill to work in the offices of the East India Company."

Diana could not believe that she was the author of her own unhappiness and wondered if it was too late to persuade Maxwell that he did not need to travel to the other side of the world in response to some unthinking words of hers early in their acquaintance. But he had not finished. "I do not expect you to wait for me, and I do not flatter myself that you have any reason to do so. But when I return to England, if you have not married, I would dearly love to call upon you as you've so kindly invited me to. I know that you have decided *not* to marry again, but I think as time passes and the memories of your first unhappy marriage recede, that perhaps you'll reconsider your decision. I wish I could be here when you do, but I anticipate being away for two or three years at least, and I imagine by the time I return, you'll have already started a new family." He looked extremely sad as he said this, heartbroken in fact, as if he was already envisioning her marriage to another man and picturing her future children, whom some other man would father.

Before Diana could gather her tumultuous thoughts, they were interrupted by one of the herds of cows that frequented the park, which passed by with their attendant milkmaids. While it was no doubt a charming, bucolic scene, the droppings (and resulting odor) the cows left in their wake caused Diana to carefully heed Maxwell's warnings to "watch your step." They hurriedly returned to the curricle by unspoken mutual consent, Diana waving a handkerchief in front of her nose. It was an unfortunate and quite unromantic ending to their excursion, and Maxwell was aware that Jim was looking profoundly disappointed at this misstep on his idol's part.

"Might want to take 'er somewhere nice now, guv," Jim said in a lowered aside to Maxwell that was nonetheless perfectly audible to Diana. "This place smells worse than a fat old man's cheeser."

Diana, who was thankfully already holding her handkerchief, was able to hide her reaction to Jim's comment behind it, and Maxwell was left to hope that Diana didn't know that "cheeser" was a slang word for flatulence, although he realized she could probably guess what Jim meant based on the context. And the smell.

"Would you like to go to Gunter's?" Max asked Diana once he had driven away from Green Park and Diana had finally removed the handkerchief from in front of her face. However, he wasn't really in the mood to extend their time together. The thought of their upcoming separation was very painful to him, the most painful separation he'd ever been faced with, even worse than having been sent away to school at the tender age of twelve.

"I think I'd do better to return home; that is, to Regina's," Diana said, and if she'd been amused by Jim's comment she was no longer. She looked as dejected as Maxwell felt. "By the way, please leave the evening before the wedding free. Lady Gordon and I are having a ball for Regina and Lord Jerome. That is why I must go; I have to write the invitation cards. You should have yours by the end of the week."

Maxwell agreed to reserve that evening and didn't know if the prospect of dancing with Diana once more before he left her, no doubt forever, was inducive of pleasure or pain, and finally decided it caused both.

As DEPRESSED AS she was after her drive with Maxwell, Diana told herself that she had no time to mope. She had to contact her man of affairs and get him to draw up some kind of document, transferring Whitley House and fifteen thousand pounds to Mildred, while retaining River House and a suitable amount of land for her own use; and she had to begin planning the ball she was to give for Regina. Only after that could she dwell on her bleak future living alone in Twickenham, removed from all society and companionship. She supposed she would have Mildred and Lucius nearby and would occasionally see them but, though Diana could find it in her heart to pity Mildred, that did not mean she would ever prove to be a sympathetic or congenial companion. In fact, Diana was fairly sure Mildred would soon revert back to her stern, crotchety ways, once the shock of recent events had worn off.

While Diana kept her promise and did not tell Regina that Lucius was Mildred's natural son, she did tell her that Percival had cheated Mildred out of her dowry and so she had resolved to give Whitley House to Mildred, along with half of her fortune, and remove to River House.

"That is quite charitable of you, Diana," Regina said, once she'd gotten over her initial surprise. "I don't know if I would have given Mildred so much, as disagreeable as she is, but I can understand why you would prefer to leave Whitley House. How many acres did you say you have?"

"I believe it's around eighty," Diana said.

"Before you give it all away, may I speak to Jerome about where he'd like to live after our marriage? Perhaps we can buy some acreage from you and build a house of our own, on the other side of River House. The part furthest away from Mildred," Regina said, with a grin.

"Oh, Regina, that would be wonderful!" Diana exclaimed happily. It was the first time she'd felt like smiling since her conversation with Maxwell.

"Don't get too excited; I have no idea what Jerome's future plans might be. It could be that he wants to live in Lincolnshire, near our family. Though I'd be very surprised if he did," Regina said, grimacing.

Jerome came to dine with Regina and Diana that evening, and Diana left them together in the drawing room afterward for their discussion. Jerome told Regina since it was her money, it was likewise her decision. "I have no objection to Twickenham, however. I enjoyed our visit there very much, and will always have fond memories of the Sweet Walk," he said, a twinkle in his eye. Since he had taken advantage of their time alone together there to bestow upon her many of the kisses he'd withheld during their earlier engagement, Regina likewise had fond memories of the place. Those remembrances soon led them into another embrace, and it was some time later before Regina could bring Jerome back to a discussion of the subject at hand.

"Seriously, Jerome," she said, removing herself from his arms and seating herself a prudent distance away, "where would you like to live after our marriage? We could continue to rent this townhouse for the season and live the greater part of the year in Lincolnshire, if you'd prefer not to live in London year-round."

"I don't think I'd like to live in London year-round, but neither do I want to remove to Lincolnshire. Twickenham seems very tranquil, while still convenient to town," he said. "And I think you'd enjoy living near Diana, my love. And she'd enjoy your companionship as well."

"So you would be agreeable to purchasing a parcel of land from her, and building a home there?"

"It sounds idyllic; if that is what you want as well," Jerome said.

"I think I do," said Regina slowly. "But Jerome, you would have to supervise the building of it."

"Certainly, my dear. You can leave that to me, though I hope you will not be shy about giving me your input."

Not only was Regina not shy about giving her input, she immediately took out paper and pencil and she and Jerome sketched out the foundation of their future house, which the architect they later hired used as the basis for his own drawings.

Diana was thrilled to learn the next morning that Regina and Jerome were to be her neighbors. Since she had done nothing yet about transferring the title of Whitley House, Diana made the decision to sell Jerome and Regina twenty-five acres (at a very good bargain), keep twenty-five acres that adjoined their lot for herself, and give Mildred the remaining thirty, which contained Whitley House and its farm.

She met with her man of affairs the next day and he approved her plans, but suggested she speak to Mildred and Lucius before he drew up the official documents. Before she could drive down to see them, however, they surprised her by calling upon her in London.

Mildred still seemed embarrassed and awkward; she wouldn't meet Diana's eyes and was uncharacteristically quiet, and Regina soon made an excuse to leave the three of them alone together. Once she did, Diana was surprised when Lucius began to apologize. Without his fake smiles and insincere compliments, he seemed like a genuinely nice man. "I am very sorry, Mrs. Boyle," he told her. "Not only did I lie to you, but I know it was wrong for me, a man of irregular birth, to pursue a genteel lady like yourself," he said, and Mildred looked more embarrassed than ever.

"Stop; please, don't," Diana said. "Mildred explained everything, and I forgive you, Cousin Lucius. I can completely understand your mother's desire to secure your future. Please, do not denigrate yourself. You either, Mildred. While what you two schemed to do was wrong, I can understand what prompted you to do it. In fact, I'd like to make some kind of recompense for what Percival did to you."

At this Mildred finally looked up at Diana. "Will you . . . do you think . . . could Lucius perhaps stay with us at Whitley House?" she asked hopefully.

"I would like to do better than that, Mildred. I would like to make over Whitley House to you and remove to River House. Whitley House will be yours, and if you'd like your son to live there with you, that will be your decision, and yours alone. I will give you the thirty acres that surround Whitley House, but I will keep twenty-five acres for myself, and I have sold twenty-five acres to Lady Regina. However, I am restoring your dowry to you as well, with interest."

Mildred looked to be in shock. "You— I don't understand, you are giving away a large portion of your fortune to me?" she asked.

"I am *restoring* your fortune to you. You will be able to provide for yourself, and for Lucius, as you always wanted to," Diana said, smiling at the older woman.

Mildred began to cry, and Lucius went over to her and awkwardly patted her shoulder. "Thank you, Mrs. Boyle," he said.

"Please, call me Cousin Diana," she replied.

17

WHEN THE ANNOUNCEMENT of Regina's engagement to Lord Jerome appeared in the papers, Regina became even more popular than she had been before, and the ladies almost wished they were back to being social outcasts, as the door knocker never stopped. However, there was one caller who came much less frequently in the days leading up to the wedding: Maxwell Dean. Apparently he was too busy arranging his affairs for his upcoming departure to India. With the unprecedented activity taking place, it took a few days for Regina to notice Maxwell's absence and comment on it, but when she finally did and Diana told her that Maxwell was taking a position with the East India Company, Regina was extremely disappointed.

"You should have told him not to go!" Regina said, after Diana told her about the conversation in Green Park.

"I was taken completely by surprise, and then the cows came!" Diana said.

"That's a terrible excuse," Regina said, but she dissolved into giggles, and Diana, as unhappy as she was, smiled in response. When Regina had composed herself, she told Diana that she must do something to prevent Maxwell from leaving.

"I asked him to call on me! How much more forward can I be?" Diana protested.

"Diana, don't be ridiculous. You consider *that* forward behavior? Miss Jarmyn actually *proposed* to Mr. Pryce."

"In English?" Diana asked, laughing.

"He obviously understood her, at any rate. They are also marrying by special license, a few days after me and Jerome. And Miss Ballard eloped with her *hairdresser*."

"What? She had two of London's most eligible bachelors courting her; a marquis and the heir to a dukedom!" Diana said, shocked.

"Apparently it was her plan to jilt them all along; she wanted revenge on them for toying with the affections of two of her closest friends."

"Good for Miss Ballard!" Diana said.

"I agree. But my point in telling you all of this, Diana, is to make it clear that you need to go much further than merely asking Mr. Dean to call. Tell him that you love him. Propose to him. Remember when we vowed to rewrite the rules of society, and beat the gentlemen at their own game?"

"But this is not a game, Regina," Diana said sadly.

"I know, love. That is why you must be brave. And you are," Regina told her. "Look at all you've accomplished these past few months; you bearded the mysterious author of the directory in his den and upbraided him for his presumptuousness; you tracked down a group of women you'd never before met and brought us together in a united purpose; you learned to drive a curricle; you hosted a ball attended by the crème de la crème of London society; and you righted a terrible wrong done to Mildred. You've accomplished amazing things, Diana. You can do this."

"That does sound pretty impressive," Diana said, with a smile. "But you neglected to mention one of the most important things I accomplished: Lady Regina Townsend is my friend."

Regina was so touched she couldn't speak, and hugged Diana tightly in response. But the poignant moment couldn't last forever, and Regina finally broke it by saying: "Forget everything I just said about proposing to Maxwell Dean; he doesn't deserve you."

Diana once again went to the Albany dressed all in black, but this time she dispensed with the veil and with Sally, her maid. What did it matter if she lost her reputation? If Maxwell wouldn't marry her, she had no desire to marry anyone.

She knew Maxwell had been very busy in recent days, and she did not want to make the effort to go to his rooms only to find he'd already left, so she arrived even earlier than she had the first time. "He's got 'em coming at the crack of dawn," Jim said under his breath, shaking his head in disbelief. Diana pretended she hadn't heard and, following him to Maxwell's door, waited while he knocked.

"Guv'nor," Jim called, when there was no response to the knock. "It's that lie-dy you took to see the cows."

This introduction caused the door to open rather hurriedly, and Maxwell appeared; a disheveled Maxwell, but an undeniably appealing one. His hair fell in disordered waves over his forehead, and he had obviously dressed in a hurry, with no time for a cravat. Diana politely ignored the fact that his neck and part of his chest were exposed and wondered that she should feel the heat so acutely when it was not yet nine o'clock.

"Diana, please come in," he said, opening the door wide. "Is something wrong?" he asked, after shutting the door in Jim's curious face.

"Yes. Something is terribly wrong," she said. But since she was smiling at him, Maxwell was understandably confused.

"Please, sit," he said, leading her to the sofa. "What is it? How can I serve you?" he asked.

And Diana, who had thought this would be so difficult, realized she should have known Maxwell would make it easy for her. "You can marry me," she said.

"What?" he asked, looking adorably sleepy and confused.

"I love you. And if you want to be of service to me, you can marry me," Diana said, slowly and clearly.

Maxwell was standing in front of Diana, who was sitting on the sofa, and he suddenly dropped down next to her. "Is this a dream?" he said, almost to himself. "Please pardon the liberty, but I've never dreamt anything so marvelous, and I must take advantage of it while it lasts," he told Diana, and pulling her into his arms, kissed her passionately and at length.

Some time later Diana felt that she must stop him, little though she wanted to. "Maxwell, this is not a dream, and you never answered my question," she said.

"Hmmm?" he murmured, pressing a kiss on her neck which caused her to shiver and wonder why she must interrupt him when he was having such a pleasant dream. But after kissing her again he drew slightly away from her, and on his face was an expression she'd never before seen, which she could only describe as a kind of triumphant satisfaction. "Did you ask me a question?" he said. "I thought it was in the nature of a command."

"You are correct; it was a command. Didn't you pledge yourself to me on the grounds of Whitley House, and offer to serve me always?"

"I did. So I'm honor bound to abide by your command, my liege lady," he said, punctuating the delicious words with an even more delicious kiss.

"Maxwell, as much as I enjoy your kisses, I am not sure you are even aware that you're awake," Diana finally said, and forced herself to stand up from the sofa and move away from him.

He stood as well, running a hand through his hair. The gesture caused her to instinctively pat her own hair, at which point she realized that somehow her bonnet had been removed during the prior interlude and was on the floor in front of the sofa. She started to retrieve it but then quickly straightened, suddenly remembering what had happened the last time she'd bent to pick something up while alone in a room with Maxwell.

"Would you hand me my bonnet?" she asked.

"Wouldn't you rather retrieve it yourself? Your hair is already mussed beyond repair, so if we were to become . . . entangled, there would be no harm done."

"Maxwell! I begin to think Jim was right about you," Diana said, slightly shocked.

"Diana, my love, Jim was as wrong as wrong can be. I am not a master seducer; I am the one who has been seduced. By the loveliest woman in England," he said, raising her hand to his lips. "Whom I would be honored, and privileged, to have as my wife. It would be beyond anything I could even dream of," he whispered, and Diana, carefully placing her hands in *his* hair, reminded herself that she was the one calling the tune, and pulled his head down to hers.

AMONG THE ENGAGEMENT announcements printed in the papers the day of Regina's ball, there were two of particular interest to the Ladies of the Registry: Diana Boyle's to Maxwell Dean and Lady Gordon's to Monsieur de la Tour. Regina protested that this ball, which was supposed to be in honor of *her* engagement, had been shamelessly appropriated by its two hostesses.

"Not that I'm complaining, mind you. I think it's wonderful that the three of us can celebrate our engagements together," she told Lady Gordon and Diana as they stood in the receiving line, just as they had on that evening when they'd hosted their first ball together. Except now Lord Jerome stood at Lady Regina's side.

"*I* have a complaint," Jerome said. "Why am I the only one of the gentlemen forced to stand in this ridiculous line and greet dozens of people?"

"This ball is in your honor," Diana explained.

"And there will be hundreds here tonight, not dozens," Lady Gordon added. "Even Lady Jersey is coming, though she had to travel back to London to be here."

"I'm sure I will be delighted to see her," Jerome said, with his ironic smile.

"You had better say so, at any rate," Regina told him, laughing.

Many members of London society had gone to hunting

lodges and seaside spas for the summer, but there were still a surprising number of acceptances for such an unseasonable event. Even Mildred and Lucius had come, and Diana was delighted that they both had donned new finery for the occasion.

Later, as Diana waltzed with her fiancé, she said, "I don't think I ever thanked you."

"For what?" he asked.

"For your very despicable directory," she said, with a smile.

"Obviously there needs to be a second edition printed, now that so many of you ladies are off the market, so to speak."

"Maxwell! You wouldn't!" Diana said, unsure whether to laugh or frown.

"No, of course I wouldn't. I was joking," he said, whirling Diana off the dance floor and into a curtained alcove away from prying eyes. "Diana, I was very happy to resign my post with the East India Company; it killed me to even contemplate leaving you, but you do know this means I'll never be a rich man, do you not? I'm not destitute, of course, and since we will live at River House we can easily use my income and keep what is left of your fortune for our children. But I had hoped to make enough in India so that no one could ever say I married you for your money, and so I could give you all the things you deserve."

"I had more than enough money, Maxwell, and it never brought me what I truly wanted. Only you can give me that, and I hope I am deserving of it," Diana said, looking lovingly up at him.

"You have my heart, wholly and completely, whatever that is worth," he said. He still held her in his arms from their waltz, and drew back a little so that he could see her face. "I love you, Diana Boyle," he whispered.

Diana wrinkled her nose in response and Maxwell was surprised, and a little hurt, by her reaction to his declaration. Seeing him frown, she hurried to explain: "I love you, too, Max, and I thought your heart was the only thing I wanted, but I realized just now when you said my name how much I want your surname, too."

Relieved by this explanation, Maxwell pulled her to him for a quick kiss. "I will happily give you that, as well."

"And you can never give me too many kisses, of course," Diana said, "and I'd also like for us to take a wedding trip to the Lake District, as I've always wanted to go, and I'd love to have your fob, since you did tell me you planned to give it to your wife one day; and oh! What I'd really like more than anything is a little girl, or boy, with your gray-blue eyes—"

"Wait!" Max said, laughing. "You will have to tell me this another time when I can write it all down. I can see that I'll be busy! You're a greedy little thing, aren't you?"

But if his smile was any indication, he had no objection to this newly discovered flaw in Diana's character.

"I confess that when it comes to you and your love, I'm very greedy, indeed. And though people may think *you* a fortune hunter, I'm the one who has captured the richest prize."

Author's Note

WHILE MAXWELL DEAN is a product of my imagination, his directory is inspired by an actual document published in 1742. Titled *A Master-Key to the Rich Ladies' Treasury or The Batchelor's Directory*, it was compiled by "a Younger Brother." Though the author was single when it was published, he apparently had hopes of changing his status soon afterward, as he dedicated the booklet to a Miss F—n, who was listed on page 22 but who he hoped would shortly remove herself from the directory upon her marriage to him.

In the foreword, addressed "To all Widowers and Batchelors," he stated the following:

Thus Gentleman, have I in the following sheets I think, opened a fair field for action for you; a fine choice, and a fine Collection of Ladies. Open the campaign directly then yourselves, that my next may be a new set. I have one favour to beg of you, and then I take my leave; that not one of you, of what degree soever, presume to attempt the Lovely Charmer I dedicate to; as to the rest, I heartily wish you all success, and am with great respect,

Your Most Obedient Unknown,

B. M—n

Suzanne Allain is a screenwriter and the author of *Mr. Malcolm's List* and *Miss Lattimore's Letter*. She lived in New York and Beijing before returning to her hometown of Tallahassee, Florida, where she lives with her husband.

VISIT SUZANNE ALLAIN ONLINE

SuzanneAllain.com

Ready to find
your next great read?

Let us help.

Visit prh.com/nextread